THE TRAIL OF BLOOD

A DETECTIVE AGNI MITRA NOVEL

SOURABH MUKHERJEE

Srishti
PUBLISHERS & DISTRIBUTORS

Srishti Publishers & Distributors
A unit of AJR Publishing LLP
212A, Peacock Lane
Shahpur Jat, New Delhi – 110 049
editorial@srishtipublishers.com

First published by
Srishti Publishers & Distributors in 2022

10 9 8 7 6 5 4 3 2 1

Printed and bound in India

About the Author

Sourabh Mukherjee has authored a true-crime anthology named *Death Served Cold* and psychological thriller novels – *The Sinners, In the Shadows of Death* and *The Colours of Passion,* long-listed in WordToScreen, Mumbai International Film Festival, 2018.

An Electronics and Telecommunications Engineer from Jadavpur University in Kolkata, in his day-job, Sourabh works in a senior leadership role in a global technology firm. Sourabh also sits in the academic councils of several premier educational institutions in India. He has spoken in global technology summits in London and Las Vegas, as well as at events organized by Society for Data Science, Bengal Chamber of Commerce and Industry, IIFT, Symbiosis, IIT Guwahati, IIM Lucknow, Kolkata University, among others.

Sourabh speaks regularly in book fairs and literary events in different parts of India. He has won several literary awards and recognitions, including the Golden Pen Award in the Sulekha Monsoon Romance Contest (2014), Juggernaut Selects (2019), Hall of Fame in Literoma International Symposium for Literature and Festival (2020). He was awarded the Man of Excellence Award 2021 by Indian Achievers' Forum for his professional achievements and contributions to nation-building.

www : www.sourabhmukherjee.com   f : authorsourabhmukherjee

: authorsourabhmukherjee   : sourabhm_ofcl

By the same author

True Crime

Death Served Cold

Thrillers

In the Shadows of Death

The Colours of Passion

The Sinners

Short stories (E-books and Audiobooks)

The Gift

The Cookery Show and a Love Story

A Special Day

Masks

An Autumn Turmoil

The Hunt

The Death Wish

Love Beyond 22 Yards

Crime Beyond 22 Yards

Loves Lost

Appreciation for the author and his works

"Sourabh Mukherjee has emerged as one of the front-runners in Indian crime fiction over the last five years."

– *Mid-day*

"Mukherjee has left his mark on the genre."

– *Deccan Herald*

"One of the most popular writers of Indian crime fiction."

– *The Asian Age*

"*Death Served Cold* is a compelling read based on true events."

– *The Times of India*

"In *Death Served Cold*, the author explores the dark recesses of the female psyche."

– *IANS*

"*Death Served Cold* reveals shocking excesses of sadism and aggression rarely associated with women."

– *Lokmat Time*

"*The Sinners* is a thrilling work of fiction that weaves together elements of corporate warfare and personal vendetta."

– *Yahoo News*

"*The Sinners* is definitely the must-read thriller book of the year."

– *The Week*

"*The Sinners* is a gripping and riveting read."

– *Outlook*

"*The Colours of Passion* delves into an entangled mess of human relationships to reveal the dark recesses that exist amidst the glitz of the film and fashion industry."

– *The Hindu*

"*The Colours of Passion* is a gripping detective thriller delving into complexities of love and hate, and also into their psychological reasons and motives."

– *The News Now*

"Set in the city of Kolkata, *In the Shadows of Death* is a fast-paced potboiler which hooks you and keeps you glued to the plot from the very beginning."

– *The Times of India*

"With an almost Freudian understanding of how our childhood experiences influence our adult decisions, Sourabh's novel (*In the Shadows of Death)* paints a stark picture of urban life in India."

– *The Hindu*

"The theatrical finale comes as much from the extraordinary storytelling as it does from the reveal of the murderer. Mukherjee has the unerring eye of a master craftsman."

– *The Hindu*

"Just when you think you've got it all figured out as per the clues that the killer leaves like crumbs, the author throws you off the path repeatedly with the twists."

– *The News Now*

"A whodunit with several twists, *In the Shadows of Death* has elements of romance, corporate scandals, and suspense with a strong emotional undercurrent."

– *The New Indian Express*

"A heady concoction of thrill, mystery, psychology and humanity is what makes this book (*In the Shadows of Death*) such an engrossing fare."

– *Punjab Tribune*

"*In the Shadows of Death* is crisp, well-composed and there are no loose ends to irk your mind."

– *Yahoo News*

"*In the Shadows of Death* is a page turner till the end with its fluid narrative infused with twists and revelations, which constantly raise your curiosity level."

– *Zee News*

"A psychological thriller in the true sense of the phrase, *In the Shadows of Death* delves deep into the psyche of its characters."

– *The Free Press Journal*

"It is not only the adrenaline rush that ignites curiosity, but also a good storyline with a meaningful plot, and of course flawless writing that does the trick …."

– *Absolute India tabloid*

"The character of detective Agni Mitra has been rendered in a very believable and realistic fashion. The author has rummaged into the human psyche and used it as the basis for the detective's theories."

– *Tehelka News*

"Mukherjee has explored the materialistic, urban life, its turmoils and fragility of relationships."

– *World News Network*

"The novel (*In the Shadows of Death*) explores the city of Kolkata in a way few contemporary novels have attempted. The City of Joy is not just a backdrop but another character in the novel."

– *Go-Getter, Go Air in-flight magazine*

To Ma,

who introduced me to the English letters.

Prologue

2010, Netarhat

The jeep came to a halt.

Pratap Jha stepped out of the jeep quietly and gestured at the officers accompanying him to maintain silence. Much to his dismay, Jha did not have the time to have his morning cup of tea as he had to leave as soon as the phone call ended. This better be worth his time.

Such an unusual phone call! Jha thought. A few seconds into the call, Jha had wondered whether he should take the caller seriously. It seemed more like a prank. Then, he had reasoned that the chances of someone trying a joke on the police at six on a chilly January morning were remote. Also, considering the situation in the state, it would not be prudent to ignore the call and let the matter pass.

What if the caller was right? Jha wondered.

Enough lives had been lost in the area over the last few months. There was no way he could take chances, especially when there were two lives involved. Jha quickly assembled a small force and headed towards the spot that the caller had directed him to. The caller could be dealt with later, if it indeed turned out to be a prank!

It was still the wee hours of the morning. One could not see far beyond the mist that hung thick on the dense bushes that lined the road. The chill in the air made its way to the bones through layers of clothing. The odd morning birds chirped and fluttered their wings, perching on dry branches.

The eastern sky was a dull purple. It seemed the sun was hesitant to rise and flag off a new day.

How would today be any different from yesterday? Or, from any day over the last several months, for that matter? Some more landmine blasts, some more deaths, some more abductions, some more suffering, some more pain and tears. That was what life in the region had come down to.

The administration, the police, the security forces – no one escaped the wrath of the Maoists. Not even some of the local people if the Maoists suspected them of passing on information to the police or colluding with the armed forces. The headlines in the newspapers made Jha cringe every day. But eventually, he had to put on his uniform and take his team out on a new operation.

There were diverse opinions and perspectives about the movement. For Jha, those were topics of heated discussions over glasses of scotch at the club in the evenings. However, on the field, there was no room for a second opinion. No Plan B. The need to uphold the law was paramount. The need to restore order in the region was unquestionable. The need to protect the innocent and the vulnerable was all that mattered.

Jha held on firmly to his gun as he moved ahead, followed by his force that was ready for action. There was not much of cover, but the police tried to be as discrete as possible. They were hiding behind the trunks of sal and mahua trees, and at times, crawling behind the odd thorny bushes. The men were silent and there was hardly any noise, but for their heavy boots trudging on withered leaves that carpeted the chapped floor of the forest. It had been a long, hard winter in Jharkhand.

Jha signalled his men to stop as they reached a clearing in the forest. He could see the man and the couple he had held hostage. Just as the caller had said on the phone.

"Sir, good morning. This is an emergency! There's a man holding a couple hostage near Magnolia Point. He has a gun."

Jha looked at the man closely. He was in a sweater and track pants. The gun was directed at the couple. He wondered what had brought the couple there so early in the day. He could see a jeep parked some distance away behind a sal tree.

Jha wondered who these people were. *Were they tourists? Not likely. They were probably locals who worked in the forest services and stayed in one of the service bungalows not too far from the area. They might have come for a walk. But was it a good idea to come for a morning walk here, considering the present scenario?*

Jha was infamous as a trigger-happy cop, though he believed that none of those shootouts had been a matter of indiscretion. From his own perspective, every one of those shootouts had been justified. He was in no mood to add to that long list of questionable encounters. And somehow, Jha did not feel comfortable with the situation. He was thinking if there was any way to figure out what exactly was going on in the mind of the man wielding the gun.

Jha could hear their voices, but could not make out what they were saying. The man with the gun was talking constantly.

He sounded hysterical. The lady had her hands folded. It seemed to Jha that she was pleading with the intruder. The other man looked stupefied. His was the feeblest voice, which barely rose above the other two.

Jha wondered what the intruder was up to.

What was going on inside his mind? Was he going to kill them? Or was he going to abduct them and then ask for a fat ransom or the release of a comrade?

Jha turned around and gestured to his men to hold fire. No sooner had he turned around than the man fired. There was no time left for small talk – the man must have decided as he pulled the trigger. The other man took the shot on his chest and was thrown backward. Jha fired at the assailant as the other man hit the ground.

Two of his officers followed suit. Three bullets were fired. Two hit the assailant on his back and another behind his knees. The sound of gunshots echoed in the forest. The man tumbled to the ground in a heap. The birds in the branches above raised a cacophony. The woman turned in the direction where Jha and his men had come out of hiding. She looked startled. She was speechless, looking alternately at the two dead men in front of her. She fell on her knees and looked at the heavens. And then she let out a gut-wrenching wail that shook the forest out of its slumber.

As Jha and his men headed towards the clearing, she stood up shakily and turned towards them. Tears were streaming down her face. With her lips trembling, she bolted towards Jha. When he was within an arm's length, the woman pounced on him.

Jha's heart skipped several beats as he looked into her eyes. He had never seen so much of hatred and anger before. The woman started clawing at his chest hysterically, like someone possessed. In between her sobs, she kept screaming, "What did you do, officer? What the hell did you just do?"

Jha and his men were no longer sure.

"Unknowns – there were too many unknowns..." that was the only thought that kept circling in Jha's mind, as his gun slipped off his hands and landed on the ground.

1 The Nightmare

Kolkata, Present Day

Agni Mitra, Assistant Commissioner, Homicide Department, Kolkata Police, stepped onto the roof of the skyscraper. It was quite late in the evening. Not a soul was in sight.

The wind felt icy cold as it ruffled his hair. Gripping the gun firmly in his hands, Agni looked around and his eyes landed on the man at the far end of the roof. The man turned his head around at the same time, and their eyes met. Agni could see blind rage simmering in those eyes. There was a menacing scowl frozen on his face. He was bleeding from the scratches on his face and his close-shaven head, which the woman must have made. He looked ghoulish.

"Shoot me, ACP! What the fuck are you waiting for?" the man asked. Agni did not miss the mockery in his voice. The man was throwing a challenge at him.

"Stop playing games with me, you bastard!" Agni shouted as he moved ahead.

The man was now less than a foot away from Agni. "Don't get ideas. Don't force me to pull the trigger. There's no way you can escape tonight," said Agni. His eyes went to the hand the man was holding. It was the hand of a woman, her fingers wrapped around the sweaty hand of the killer, her body dangling on the other side of the railing. Agni could now see the top of her head. He could now hear her cries above the roar of the wind.

"Agni, is that you?" the woman screamed. Her hope was rekindled by the familiar voice.

"Pull her up. *Now!*" Agni screamed at the man as he took aim, the gun pointing at the man's forehead.

The only sounds were those of the wind whispering ominously and the relentless cries of the woman. The chill was getting to the bones of the two men and the woman who were brought together by destiny at that vantage point, towering over the city.

Agni could hear sirens at a distance. In no time, armed policemen would be streaming out of police cars and running towards the building.

"Your game is up! The cops are here. This is not your night," Agni said as he inched closer, the gun aimed at the man's forehead. He could now smell the man's stale breath.

"Pull her up right now," Agni said once again as he stretched his free hand towards the woman.

"Alright, supercop!" Before Agni could bat an eyelid, the man had raised both his hands in the air.

"I surrender," the man said, and then turned towards the railing, almost as an afterthought.

"Oops! I forgot your wife. My condolences, officer!" His eerie, phlegmy laughter filled the night.

"Fuck you!" Agni screamed as he ran towards the railing. He could hear heavy boots on the roof. The cops lost no time in taking positions around the man, their guns trained firmly at him.

Agni bent over the railing and he saw his wife's receding figure rush through the chilly air of the night towards the empty road shrouded by fog, hundreds of feet below. Her arms were stretched, her mouth was wide open, her hair blown by the wind formed a halo around her head and the fear of imminent death was frozen in her eyes.

"Medha!" Agni cried out in despair.

❖

Agni's hand was still trying to grasp thin air when he sat up and looked around his dark room. He closed his eyes, waiting for the last traces of the nightmare to disappear. His throat was dry and his lips were parched. His breath reeked of the whiskey from last night.

Then, he reached for the glass of water on the nightstand and finished it in one gulp. He got off the bed and made his way wearily to the bathroom. He splashed cold water on his face and neck, and ran his wet fingers through his hair. He kept looking at his reflection in the mirror.

"Five years…five fucking years," he reminded himself. "She's been gone five years now. There's absolutcly nothing that you could've done that night."

A voice deep inside him protested.

But you were simply getting wasted in a bar! You could have dropped by her house much earlier, before the killer got her! You could have taken a shorter route! You could have driven faster. The roads were deserted, for god's sake! Above all, why the fuck did you let her walk out on you and start living alone in the first place? You could have pleaded with her to stay back. You loved her, didn't you?

Agni squeezed his eyes shut and closed his ears with his hands. But the voice would not go away. It had not, for the last five years.

Images flashed in front of Agni's eyes – the sparse midnight traffic on a rain-washed Red Road as he drove towards Medha's house, light-headed after the heavy drinking throughout the evening; knocking frantically on Medha's door and calling her on the phone, the only ominous response being the incessant ringing of her mobile phone inside the house; and then breaking into her house to find her dead in her bedroom in the buff, strangled by the deranged serial killer whom Agni had been chasing.

Agni shut his eyes tighter and his jaws stiffened, as the blood-red words on the wall of Medha's dining hall glared back at him from the dark chambers of his memory – the letters still wet, the red making long trails down the wall.

Agni, don't take this personally

He could still hear his own guttural scream that had reverberated in the empty house and pierced through the cold silence of the night. He had lost Medha forever. A part of him had also died that night.

Agni splashed more water on his face, trying desperately to wipe off the sinister memories and walked back to his bedroom. He dragged the heavy curtains aside. The sky had already started clearing. He looked at the bottle of whiskey. A third of it was still full. He needed the whiskey to numb his pain and get some sleep.

He was about to pick up the bottle when his phone buzzed. Agni picked it up with a deep furrow between his brows.

It was Inspector Arya Sen.

2 A New Case

Agni walked in through the gate of the bungalow in a desolate part of New Town. There were not too many houses in the vicinity, none of the office complexes that this part of the city was known for, not much traffic either at that hour of the day.

He looked up to see Arya approaching him along the immaculately maintained lawn. Agni looked around. There was a car in the garage to his right. It was a black BMW. The lawn led to a two-storeyed bungalow. There were potted plants hanging along a small balcony on the first floor. An ivy made its way up the wall to that balcony. All the windows facing the lawn were presently closed.

"Who called the police?" asked Agni as he walked up the stairs, Arya leading the way.

"Her attendant. The bodies, however, were seen first by her cook Pratima. They sleep downstairs. Pratima had come up in the morning to serve tea," Arya replied.

Arya reached the top of the staircase and turned left. He stopped in front of a room. "Here we are, Agni. This is the master bedroom. When we came in, there was just the light on the nightstand. Next to this is the drawing room with a bar. It opens to a kitchen and a small dining space. The doctor is here and the forensics are already on the job."

It took Agni a few seconds to take in the spectacle in front of his eyes.

Singer Deboleena Mukherjee was sprawled on her back on the bed in her dressing gown, her legs reaching down to the floor. Her eyes were closed. It did not look like death had caused her a lot of pain. Facing her, sitting on a chair with his back to the door was a man. His head drooped to a side. He had been shot on his left temple. The face had been reduced to a bloody mess.

The wall on the other side had been sprayed with fragments of bones, brain, hair and a lot of blood that streamed down the wall. There was blood everywhere. The man's untucked shirt was blood-soaked. His blood was on the floor. There were bloodstains on the coat that was hung around the back of the chair.

Between the two corpses was a low table. There was a bottle of wine and two empty glasses, all of which were shortly picked up by the forensics. On the table was a plateful of roasted cashew nuts. There was a drinks trolley next to the table.

"What about her family?" Agni turned towards Arya.

"She was a widow. Her elder brother, Debesh Roy lives at the other end of the town, in Tollygunge. Ms Mukherjee's attendant informed him earlier this morning."

"Do we know who this gentleman is?" Agni asked, pointing at the dead man.

"Not yet. We will look for his ID."

"Is that Ms Mukherjee's car in the garage?"

"Yes, it is. I checked with the servants."

Agni nodded. "Doc, how long ago do you think the murders took place?" he asked the doctor who was examining the corpses.

"Both of them died around the same time. Around seven hours ago. Of course, we will have more exact timings when we do the autopsy."

"So, this happened around twelve last night," Agni looked at his watch. It was close to seven in the morning.

"How do you think Ms Mukherjee died?"

"Looks like she had a cardiac arrest. We will need to figure out what caused it. The autopsy should tell us more," the doctor said.

Agni turned towards Arya and said, "Don't you think it's rather unusual that there are two corpses in the *same* room but strangely, there are two different kinds of death? One of them died from a cardiac arrest, while the other was shot at." Arya nodded in agreement, looking confused.

Agni looked around the room. There was affluence and fine taste written all over. The wallpapers had azure skies, lush green forests and waterfalls. There was a television on the wall facing the bed. The other walls were almost completely hidden behind bookcases. Agni noticed that there was a harmonium and a sitar in one corner of the room.

There was an attached toilet, the door of which was left ajar. Agni walked up to the toilet and pushed the door slightly. He looked at the window. It was intact. There was no sign of a break-in. There was a balcony on the other side of the room. The door leading to the balcony was open. Agni tiptoed his way to the door around the forensics who were busy taking pictures or picking up evidence with gloved hands and putting them in plastic bags.

Agni walked onto the balcony. Arya joined him. Agni bent over the railing and looked down. The balcony overlooked the lawns at the back of the house. The lawns extended to a boundary wall.

He turned to Arya and said, "We must make sure that the house and the premises are searched thoroughly. I don't rule out the possibility of someone coming in from outside. It must not have been difficult for someone to scale that wall, run down the lawn, climb up to this balcony and get into the room!

"Here, look at that rain pipe that runs right next to the balcony. If this door had been left open all night, which I believe was the case, the killer must have left along the same route as well. We should check with all the police stations in this area if anyone noticed anything unusual last night. Also, let's check all the traffic cameras around this place."

"Yes, we will do all of that. But, let me ask you something. Even if we assume that the killer entered the room this way, would the killer not be easily seen by the two persons inside the room? And had the killer been seen, they would have shouted for help, they would have been heard by the servants downstairs and there should have been signs of struggle in the room. Right now, nothing looks out of place inside this room. I checked with the servants and apparently, they heard nothing unusual last night."

"You may be right, Arya. But, think of this. The only other way to enter this room is through the door at the top of the staircase – the one we came in through. We will need to check with the servants if they let anyone in through the main door of the bungalow around the time of the murder. Or perhaps, saw or heard anyone climbing the stairs.

"If they did not, then this is the only way left for the killer to enter the room. In that case, the very facts that there was no resistance, no one screamed for help or alerted the servants downstairs, suggest that the killer was not seen. The big question is 'why'!"

3 Hotel Paradise

Agni walked into the spacious living room downstairs. A sofa set was spread out in the middle of the room, with a central table in front. There were a few magazines on the table. The television was on the wall facing the sofa. There was a wall clock fixed right above the television. Adjacent to the main door, there was a bookcase that rose close to the ceiling. At the other end of the room, there was a dining table and a refrigerator.

There was a curtain that separated the sitting area from the dining area. The curtain was presently drawn aside. The dining table was next to a window. It was closed and the curtains were drawn, just as they had been the night before. Agni figured out that the window opened to the backyard. Facing the dining area was a kitchen which had a door that led to the back of the house. The door was presently closed.

Pratima was the first to walk in. She appeared to be in her mid-forties.

Agni asked her, "Did you see the bodies first?"

Pratima was clearly shaken by the ghastly sight she had woken up to. She looked pale, her hands and lips trembled and she stammered as she spoke.

"Y...Yes."

"Why did you go upstairs?"

"I... I go there every day. I used to bring madam her morning tea."

"Even when she had guests?"

Pratima was quiet for a while and then she said, "She hardly had guests staying overnight. Madam is... er, was a famous singer. She obviously had lots of visitors through the day when she was home. She also had friends from the industry. But they never stayed till late."

"When did madam come home last night?"

"It was around ten. We had just finished dinner and I was going to bed."

"Did you actually see madam coming in?"

Pratima again hesitated, and then muttered, "No. I heard her car. She has her own keys. She used them whenever she returned late. She did not want us to stay awake."

"Did she have dinner at home last night?"

"No."

"Was that normal?" Agni asked.

"No. She usually had dinner at home. But yesterday, she called Manoj in the evening and said that she would not have dinner. She also told him that she would be late and we should not stay up."

"Did you know that she had returned home last night with a gentleman?" Agni asked suspiciously.

Pratima was silent. Her eyes were downcast.

"Answer my question," he asserted.

"I heard voices upstairs, but I wasn't sure. Manoj told me this morning that he had seen madam going up with a gentleman."

"Did you see or hear anything unusual anytime during the night? Gunshots? Screams?"

Pratima said, "No. I heard music for some time, which was normal. I heard voices from upstairs as I told you just now. And then, I fell asleep."

"Did anyone else come later in the night?"

"No one, sir."

"Did you, by any chance, see anyone in the backyard, or heard anything there?"

Pratima again thought for a while and shook her head in the negative.

"You can go now."

Pratima stood up to leave. Agni told her, "Don't leave this house, till the time you're told otherwise. Send in Manoj."

❖

Manoj was in his early thirties. He seemed to be in better control of his faculties and was willing to volunteer information. He narrated a similar story. He had, however, seen Deboleena with her guest.

"I was awake when madam's car rolled in. I heard the door open and then, I heard voices. That was very unusual. Madam hardly had guests, and definitely not so late in the night! At first, I thought I had made a mistake. Then, I heard heavy steps on the staircase. I heard a man's voice. I heard the two of them laughing. I'll be honest with you, sir. My curiosity got the better of me. I opened the door of my room and peeped outside. My room is right at the bottom of the staircase. I could see madam climbing the stairs with a man."

"Did you manage to see his face?"

"I'm afraid I didn't, sir. They were climbing up the stairs, and I managed to see them only from the back."

He stopped abruptly. Agni had the feeling that he wanted to say more, but was hesitant for some reason.

"Is there anything else you want to tell me?"

Manoj smiled sheepishly and said, "Well... I've been working here for more than six years. I had never seen madam come home in the company of a man, or entertain a male friend in the house late in the evening. To be honest, I was rather shocked! I didn't get any sleep for a while. My mind was disturbed, I guess."

"Did you hear or see anything unusual after they had gone upstairs? Anywhere in the house or in the backyard?"

"I heard their voices upstairs. You know, talking and laughing. Madam put on the music for some time. She did that every night before going to bed," Manoj paused briefly and said, "and as for the backyard, the doors and windows facing the backyard remain closed at night."

"Did you let anyone else in through the main door at any time during the night, after Ms Mukherjee had arrived?"

"No. Madam was the last one to come in, with her friend."

"Did she have any other visitor yesterday?"

Manoj thought for a while and said, "Her brother, Debesh sir had come in the morning. He drops by frequently to check on her."

"Can you think of anyone else who visited her frequently?"

"No one else in particular," Manoj paused briefly and said, "but Tarun sir, madam's lawyer, used to visit her sometimes."

"Alright! Do you have his contact number?"

"Yes, sir. I do. I'll give you Tarun sir's number."

"Was it you who informed Ms Mukherjee's brother about her death this morning?"

"Yes, sir. I did. I called him as soon as Pratima came down from madam's room and told me what she had seen."

"What did Mr Roy say?"

"He said that he would be here right away. But he hasn't turned up yet..."

The conversation was interrupted by Arya stepping into the room.

"Agni, you must see these!" Arya looked excited.

He stretched out a gloved hand holding two plastic bags. He had picked them up from the forensics team working upstairs.

Inside one, there was a key card. Inside the other, there was a driving license.

"We found these on the man. The key card was in his trousers' pocket. The driving license was in his wallet."

"This looks like the key card of a hotel," Agni said. "Hotel Paradise." He brought the card closer to his eyes and read the address of the hotel. "It's on E.M. Bypass. I think I know the place."

Then, he picked up the plastic bag with the driving license and read the name on it.

Avigyan Chowdhury. Thirty-five years old.

He looked at the picture. Square jaw, sharp features, hair parted to a side – easy on the eyes. He turned to Arya and said, "This license has an address in Mumbai."

"That means, Avigyan came on a visit to Kolkata and put up in Paradise."

Agni showed the picture on the driving license to Manoj. He said that he had never seen the man before. Avigyan Chowdhury had never visited that house before last night.

Agni turned to Arya and said, "We will need to make enquiries at the hotel. But before that, I need some breakfast. I'm starving."

4 | The Worst Enemy

Kolkata, 2003

Someone told me a few days back that if you are really messed up in your mind, and the voices you hear inside your head round the clock become unbearable, it is best to start looking back at your life. You think in a more structured manner, as you analyse everything that you have gone through. It also gives you a fresh perspective. You see facts and details staring at you that you did not notice earlier. It also helps you feel lighter and drift off to sleep more easily.

Sleep! It costs you nothing, yet it could be your most elusive craving.

A lot of us have the notion that each one of us is born with a certain character. That's bullshit. We are born like a gooey lump of clay. Then, our environment shapes us. Our parents, our upbringing and our conscious and unconscious experiences shape our ways of thinking and our behaviour, basically making us who we are. Coming to think of it, we become who we are, without being able to control any of these factors. Isn't that a scary thought?

How much was I to blame for what I became?

I realized early in my childhood that my father had an anger management issue. At the slightest provocation, he would bring the house down. He would throw things around. He would beat my mother and leave her bruised all over. I would not be spared on most occasions, unless I managed to hide somewhere or run away from the house through the back door. I would invariably wet my pants as he would whip me mercilessly with his leather belt or a stick, or for that matter, anything he found handy. The pain from the flogging would keep me up night after night. I would keep hearing his voice echoing inside my small, dark room, long after he had beaten me black and blue, emptied a bottle of cheap liquor and dozed off.

No one in the family denied that he was hopelessly mad, but no one did anything about it. The result was that my childhood became a never-ending nightmare, scarred by pain, tears and the pathetic sight of broken articles around the house.

As I grew older, even if the scars on my body healed, deep inside I was a weak, vulnerable child who feared the world and had an extremely poor opinion of himself. I was that child who never mustered the courage to stand up for himself, to demand what was rightfully his. Instead, he would hide from everyone and make crooked plans of stealing whatever he fancied. I was growing up to be an imperceptible shadow lurking in the dark, my twisted mind scheming and plotting as I was too scared to come out in the light.

I used to think that if I could get out of that madhouse, I would be fine. I believed that there was a world outside – warm, pretty, colourful – that would welcome me with open arms, the day I stepped out of my house of horrors. So, I grabbed the first opportunity to leave my family when I got the chance to study commerce at a college in Kolkata.

My father could not care less. My mother was scared that she would be the only one left in the house to endure my father's wrath. I felt sorry for her. But I did not allow my love for my mother to get in the way of my resolve. That was the freedom I had craved for, all through my abused childhood and troubled adolescence.

❖

I reached Kolkata and joined college. I stayed in the college hostel for boys, not very far from the campus. I had an uncle who lived in Kolkata, but the last time he had seen me was when I was three. He had walked away from the family years back, just like I did. He had nothing much to do with my parents, barring the customary greetings for Durga Puja and the Bengali New Year. My mother had informed him that I was going to be in Kolkata for my studies, and apparently, he had said that I could stay with him. But I was not too keen on being a pile on, and had made up my mind that I would ask for his help only if there was no other option left.

However, it did not take me too long to realize that I had been completely wrong about how running away from my father would change my life. I had not left my demons behind; they were right inside me.

My father's voice kept echoing in my ears, reminding me all the time that I was weak and worthless. I could not make friends easily. I could not socialize. I could not join the boys when they played on the grounds, or when they went for late-night movies, or when they drank cheap rum on the roof of the boys' hostel, or when they ogled at porn magazines. I was trapped inside, and I would not set myself free.

I was my worst enemy.

5 | Bad News

Kolkata, Present Day

Paradise was located on the Eastern Metropolitan Bypass, a few hundred meters from Science City. The hotel had clearly seen better days. It was one of those hotels which had come up in the area a few years back, with plans of recovering investment from business travellers because of their proximity to the IT hub of the city. But now, it was being outrun by global chains who had not taken long to discover the potential of the region.

Paradise was now trying hard to stay afloat by letting out rooms by the hour to couples who would rather not display identity proof for an afternoon romp or to hookers who needed a safe haven for running their business. There was also a bar on the first floor, hidden from the traffic on the Bypass by thick dark glasses, with a 'Live Band Every Night' advertised.

Agni wondered what form of entertainment was offered live inside that bar. He, along with Arya, walked up to the reception.

The air-conditioner was barely functional. There was a balding man in a white shirt and a black coat. He seemed lost in his mobile phone, looking genuinely bored. The coat sat tight on his opulent frame. The fat around his chin and jaws hung past his stiff collar. There were large sweat patches on his chest.

Behind the reception desk, there was a painting depicting a rural scene – a well-endowed village belle wrapped in a white saree and an excuse of a blouse that barely covered her ample breasts, carrying water from a river that was painted red by the rising sun as a couple of cows looked on in bovine wonder. Under the glaring light from a couple of overhead lamps, the dust on the painting was prominent.

Agni heard the sound of heels and turned around to see a girl in a clingy top and short skirt, her hair pulled back, her cheap face-paint peeling off with the sweat. She walked in through the glass door and sashayed her way to the lift. She threw a coquettish glance at the men. The man at the reception did not bother to look up from his phone.

Agni finally tapped on the reception desk to draw the man's attention.

The man said, without looking up, "Night-stay or by-the-hour?"

Agni did not answer his question. Instead, he pulled out his ID and passed it across the desk.

The man took his eyes off the phone and threw a cursory glance at the card. In the very next moment, he transferred the phone to a drawer. He stood in attention, ran his fingers along his damp scalp, cleared his throat, and asked, "Hello sir, my name is Ujjwal. What would you like, sir? Tea, coffee, Pepsi?"

Agni asked, "Do you have a guest by the name of Avigyan Chowdhury staying in the hotel?"

Ujjwal pulled out a fat register. He went to the page with the last few entries and ran his finger down the names. He finally stopped at one. "Yes sir, here it is. Avigyan Chowdhury. Isn't that the name?"

"It sure is," said Agni. "When did he check in?"

Ujjwal went back to the entry in the register and said, "He checked in yesterday around noon, sir. He had a booking for a night. But I'm wondering... he hasn't checked out yet. He was supposed to check out at eleven. Maybe I'll send someone up to his room to check if he's planning to extend his stay..."

In the meantime, the conversation at the reception had drawn the manager out from a glass cabin to the left. The manager was an emaciated man in an ill-fitting suit, his oil-slick hair brushed back. Agni greeted the manager with a nod and continued with his questioning.

Ujjwal turned briefly towards the manager and said, "Sir, they are from Kolkata Police."

Agni acknowledged the greetings of the manager and turned down yet another offer of tea or coffee or Pepsi. He asked Ujjwal, "Did you see this guest leave the hotel any time last night?"

"Yes, sir. I remember seeing him leave the hotel last night with a woman."

"A *woman*? Was she staying in this hotel as well?"

"No, sir. Mr Chowdhury had called me in the evening saying that he was expecting a guest – a lady. He said that he would wait for her in the bar upstairs and when she arrived, she was to be sent there."

"When did the lady arrive?"

"I'm sorry I don't remember the exact time, sir. It must have been around seven or half-past seven."

"And when did you see the two of them leaving the hotel?"

"That would be around nine, sir."

"Did you or anyone else see him return?"

"I'm not sure, sir. I don't do night shifts."

"Do you remember how they left the hotel?"

"In the lady's car, sir. We have valet parking and I remember the lady asking for her car to be fetched."

Agni nodded.

"Was the bill from the bar settled?"

"No. sir. It was charged to the room..."

"I would like to see the invoice."

"Sure, sir."

Ujjwal searched in a drawer and pulled out a signed invoice. Agni went through it. Dinner and six glasses of whiskey. He passed the invoice on to Arya.

Agni turned towards the manager and said, "We'll keep this invoice."

"Sure, sir...any problem, sir?" The manager looked concerned.

"Well...your guest was murdered last night, and he isn't coming back to check out, or pay for the food and the whiskey."

The manager gulped and kept looking at Agni incredulously. Arya wondered if the rulebook had a method for recovering dues from a murdered guest. The manager finally muttered a barely audible "Oh!"

Agni turned towards Arya and said, "Arya, make sure we seal the room and run a thorough search in it with the help of the forensics. We'll also need to look at CCTV footages – front, lobby area, the floor where Avigyan stayed, elevators and the bar.

❖

As Agni and Arya walked out of Paradise, Arya's phone rang. As he listened to the caller, his face grew dark. When he ended the call, Agni turned towards him and asked, "What is it?"

"I have bad news, Agni. Ms Mukherjee's elder brother – Mr Roy – suffered a heart attack as soon as he received the news of her death this morning. He is in a hospital."

"This means we would not be able to talk to Mr Roy anytime soon." Agni sighed.

6 Call Records

Agni sat inside his office poring over a bunch of papers. His brow was creased, and he did not notice when Arya had come in.

Arya cleared his throat to announce his arrival. Agni gestured to him to take a seat and looked up from the papers.

"Agni, we have call records from the last three months for both the phones," said Arya.

"First tell me about the call records from the day of the deaths," said Agni.

"Let me start with Avigyan's records. There are two numbers to which Avigyan made calls after reaching Kolkata. One of them is Ms Mukherjee's. We will need to find out who the other number belongs to. Then, there are sundry calls he made to cab drivers, the Paradise hotel and the like. We also found an e-ticket in his phone. He had planned to return to Mumbai the very next day. He was in Kolkata just for that night."

"Did you find anything useful in his hotel room?"

"Nothing that might be of interest, Agni. His change of clothes, some money and travel papers."

"Alright," Agni nodded. "Let us come back to the call logs. What about Ms Mukherjee's call records from the day?" asked Agni.

"There is something rather unusual about that. Her brother, Mr Roy, called her *twenty-seven times!*"

Agni sat up straight. "You have Ms Mukherjee's call records from the last three months. I assume that was not normal."

"It wasn't at all. You must also remember that, according to Manoj, Mr Roy and Ms Mukherjee had met in the morning on the same day!"

"It would be interesting to find out what the two of them had talked about that morning. Something that had led to twenty-seven follow-up calls during the rest of the day," Agni said thoughtfully. Then, he asked, "What else do we see in Ms Mukherjee's records?"

"There are a couple of calls to Avigyan's number during the afternoon. They probably made plans for the evening. There's one in the evening around seven. That was probably made when she reached the hotel, as the receptionist mentioned. There's one that was made to her residence earlier in the evening, probably to inform the servants that she would be late and would not have dinner at home. This was also mentioned by Manoj, if you recall. Then, there are a few calls which have been tracked to musicians and producers she worked with."

Arya paused briefly and then said, "Avigyan and Ms Mukherjee had spoken twice before Avigyan came down to Kolkata. The first call had been made by Ms Mukherjee and the second by Avigyan. We also checked their activities on social media. Interestingly, they became friends on Facebook just a couple of weeks back!"

Agni closed his eyes and said, "Avigyan came down to Kolkata from Mumbai, put up at Paradise with a booking for only one night. However, he chose to spend the night with Ms Mukherjee. Was that always the plan or did they decide to spend the night together when they met in the evening? Did they meet each other on Facebook, and then decided to meet in person in Kolkata, only to be killed on their first night together?"

There was silence in the room for a while. Then, Agni asked, "Anything else, Arya?"

Arya said, "Ms Mukherjee taught music in a few schools. I spoke to the students and the other teachers. They had not noticed anything unusual in her behaviour over the last few weeks. The same observations came from the producers and composers with whom she had been working. She usually kept to herself and was not very sociable. It seems there are very few people who knew her really well." Arya paused briefly and asked, "What had you been looking at when I came in?"

"The post-mortem reports have come in, Arya. Together with the forensic reports, they are quite intriguing!"

7 | Speculations

Agni stood up from his seat and started walking around his desk. "Ms Mukherjee had taken an overdose of sedatives. Consumed above safety limits with alcohol, it proved to be fatal. As for Avigyan, and this is what I find quite baffling, an overdose of the *same* sedative was also detected in his viscera!"

Agni paused briefly.

"On top of that, he was also shot at," Arya thought aloud, "while Ms Mukherjee was not!"

"Exactly! They found a gunshot entry wound on the left side of Avigyan's skull. The forensics found the bullet next to the body, slightly deformed and deviated in its trajectory as it penetrated through the other side of his skull.

"His skull had split open. We did find some of his brain matter on the wall, remember? As per reports, he was shot by a 0.32 calibre pistol. They found particles of gunpowder embedded in the skin. There was also skin burn, potentially from the hot exhaust gases from the barrel. These observations prove beyond doubt that he was shot at from fairly close range.

"Interestingly, traces of the same sedative that was present in the viscera of Avigyan and Ms Mukherjee, were also found in the wine glasses that they drank from. Forensics found an empty bottle of sleeping pills in Ms Mukherjee's kitchen cabinet. It is the same sedative that was found in the bodies of Avigyan and Ms Mukherjee. It is a drug that cannot be purchased over the counter."

"What are your thoughts about the killer?" Arya looked confused.

"It seems quite unlikely to me that anyone inside the house shot Avigyan. The killer must have come into the room from outside and shot Avigyan in the head. I explained to you the other day that since there was no break-in and the servants did not let anyone in through the main door after Ms Mukherjee and Avigyan had arrived that night, the only way the killer could have come in was over the boundary wall, across the lawn, up the rain-pipe, and then into the room through the balcony."

"But, neither Avigyan nor Ms Mukherjee saw the killer," said Arya.

"Yes, none of them saw the killer, *because both of them were unconscious*! There can be no other explanation. They had consumed the wine with the sleeping pills, *before* the killer came in."

"So, you're saying that the killer did not know that the two of them had already taken a lethal overdose of sleeping pills? Why else would the killer still go ahead and shoot the guy in the head?"

"Put yourself in the shoes of the killer, Arya. You are out to kill someone. You enter a room and find your target in the company of a woman, with two wine glasses and a bottle of wine in front of him. They have been drinking and apparently, they are asleep. There is no way for you to figure out that they have actually taken an overdose of a sedative that would kill them anyway. What would you do? You would simply do your job and leave."

"What if the killer already *knew* that the two were unconscious? Maybe they were *meant* to pass out before the killer came in so that they won't see the killer," countered Arya.

"Well, that's also a possibility," agreed Agni. "Though, in that case, it would have been enough to make the two simply pass out, not *die* from a lethal overdose of that drug."

"No one heard the gunshot!"

"The killer must have used a silencer. He finished his job and went back along the same route out of the house."

"Interestingly, the killer knew where to find Avigyan that night, even though Avigyan had booked into Paradise," Arya said. "Now, based on what we know so far, the only two persons who knew where Avigyan would be that night were Ms Mukherjee and Avigyan himself unless one of them had discussed the plan with someone else. If we rule out that possibility for a moment, then it seems logical that Ms Mukherjee was the one who had hired a professional killer. What do you think?"

"That's certainly possible. There is another possibility, though. The killer might have been shadowing Avigyan through the day and he had just followed him to Ms Mukherjee's house that night," said Agni.

8 | The One

Kolkata, 2004

I saw Deboleena for the first time in our college fest. I usually dreaded going to fests. There would be boys and girls – smart, confident, good-looking – performing on stage, making new friends, hanging out in groups, and generally, having a great time.

I did not fit in. I could not dream of getting up on stage and making a fool of myself. I never managed to muster the courage to walk up to a girl and strike a conversation. I was acutely conscious of my roots, my bad English and my cheap clothes. Therefore, I avoided my classmates, sneaked into the auditorium, sat among strangers, and watched the performances. Deep inside, I was consumed by unbridled envy for every boy and girl who sang or performed in a skit or acted in a play. I used to keep telling myself that I could do better than any of them. But I never had the courage to give myself a chance.

Deboleena won the inter-college singing contest for girls. As she sang on stage, the mellifluous notes floating in the auditorium mesmerized the audience. I could barely breathe. It seemed as if someone had sucked the air out of my innards. That very moment, I knew that was it. She was the one, and there would never be another all my life.

Over the next several weeks, I followed Deboleena, wherever she went in the campus – keeping my distance, hiding behind crowds of boys and girls. I felt exhilarated just by being close to her, in the very act of following her around. It felt as if a secret door had opened up and Deboleena, with her arms open, had seduced me into crossing a threshold and stepping into a colourful, warm, magical world that I had never known existed.

I was in love.

Here was finally the special connection with another human being that I had longed for all my life. I had started to believe that I was too broken, too damaged to ever feel love and attraction for another human being. But I was proved wrong. Deboleena proved me wrong.

As I watched her from a distance, when she laughed, I could feel a wave of happiness surge through me. When I saw her upset, I was surrounded by a pall of gloom. I wanted to break away from the chains with which I had tied myself. I wanted to stand in front of her and tell her that she was the most precious gift that god had ever blessed me with. I would do anything to take care of her till my last breath. I wanted to see her happy. I wanted to make her feel special and love her like no human being had ever loved another.

❖

I had the script ready. I had written and re-written it and had rehearsed in all sincerity in front of the mirror inside the dirty toilet in the boys' hostel. But it would not take long for me to remind myself of where I came from, the way I spoke, the way I dressed. Convincing myself that I would never manage to win her heart was simple, especially when I looked at the boys she usually hung out with. They were smart and suave, rich kids who came to college in trendy cars and had lunch in expensive restaurants outside the campus.

After months of languishing, I finally decided to make a move. It was the last day of our semester examinations. I had turned up in a crisp white shirt, tucked neatly into a pair of black trousers – my best attire which I had kept reserved for campus interviews. I made my way through boisterous boys and girls flocking out of the examination hall and stood in front of her. My throat was dry, my lips were parched and my palms were sweating.

"I wanted to have a word with you," I walked up to Deboleena gingerly and said as per the script, as she walked out of the examination hall.

"Do I know you?" Deboleena looked up at me. She had the beauty that could dazzle the eyes, pride that was intimidating, and voice that was lilting.

"You probably don't know me. I am in the commerce department. I heard you sing in the fest and ..."

"That was over three months back! Isn't this a bit late for compliments?" she exclaimed and broke into a laughter. Two other girls joined her. I hated them immediately.

"I... well ..." I was lost for words. I began stammering. My natural accent was threatening to break free. I said, "I've been

preparing for the semesters, you know, and could not make time to meet you..."

"You're a very sincere student, I have to say!" Deboleena said. More laughter followed. "Thanks a lot, anyway. You have anything else to tell me?"

I wished I could tell her that I could lay down my life for her that very moment. That she was the reason why life had found a new meaning. That she was the reason why my world was drenched in colours I had never seen.

All I managed to say was, "I was wondering if we can get to know each other... I love music too..."

"That's very nice. Do you sing?" Deboleena gestured to her friends to stop giggling. By now, I wanted to strangle those two girls.

"No... I don't sing," I mumbled.

There was an awkward silence and the three girls exchanged glances.

I said, "Listen... I was heading towards the canteen. Are you girls hungry?"

Deboleena looked at her friends and said, "Yes, we won't mind a snack."

I thought that was sweet of her. In fact, I took that for a small victory.

I ordered cutlets for all four of us, shouting above the ruckus of boys and girls who crowded the payment counter. It was my most expensive purchase in the canteen till date. Deboleena insisted that we take the food away, as she was in a hurry. If my spirits ebbed, I tried my best not to show.

She let me walk with her to the gates of the college. We talked about our schools, the music we heard, and how she spent time at home playing her grandmother's piano. When I gathered all the courage in the universe and asked for her phone number, she refused. "In fact, don't ever think of calling me. My parents are very strict. Don't worry! I'm sure we'll bump into each other in the campus," those were her parting words.

There was a car waiting for her outside the campus. She got into that car with the two girls, and the car sped away, leaving a cloud of dust in its trail. I kept looking at that car till it vanished around the bend.

I kept grinning as I walked towards the hostel. It seemed to me that I had won the biggest battle of my life. It seemed that the world around me was new and beautiful. Deboleena Roy had permitted me not only to buy cutlets for her and her friends, but also to walk with her up to the college gate!

The vacation started and for the first time, I could not wait for college to reopen. When it finally did, I ran to the arts department, and tried to decipher the very complicated class routine that had been put up on the notice board, just to figure out what would be the best time to drop by and meet Deboleena.

However, contrary to Deboleena's words of solace, our paths did not cross for the next few weeks. I wondered if the timings of her classes had changed. I wondered if she was sick. I wondered if she had left the college.

❖

I finally ran into her after a month and a half. It was a sultry afternoon. I had bunked my own classes after recess as I waited outside the arts building.

She emerged like a vision, with the same girls in tow, making her way towards the library. I ran up to her and stood panting, a couple of feet away from her, struggling to find my words. I was almost in tears with happiness and gratitude. Also, I had not thought about what I would say if she asked me what I was doing in the arts building at that time of the day. At the same time, all the emotions bottled up inside my chest for all those weeks were trying to break free. I wanted to tell her how much I had missed her during the holidays and the weeks thereafter, and how happy and blessed I felt to see her.

She almost did not notice me. But then, our eyes met. All I read in those eyes was faint remembrance. I probably looked familiar to her – one of the many boys in the campus who flocked around her. Her lips curled in a half-smile, and she walked away with her friends, never stopping her animated conversation with the two girls. My heart sank and I felt light-headed. I realized that I had been sweating profusely, and probably presented a rather sorry sight.

In the weeks that followed, I ran into her a few more times, inside the campus, and once, at the bus stop. On both occasions, I tried to engage in small talk with a lot of difficulty. My natural lack of spontaneity was further aggravated by her indifference and ice-cold demeanour.

On both occasions, she spoke to me politely, but I did not miss the lack of interest and her keenness to ward me off with unconvincing excuses, mostly about how busy she was with impending examinations and music classes.

❖

The next few months were agonizing.

When the next semester examinations started, I waited outside the arts building on the first day for an hour so that I would not miss her. I wanted to wish her luck for her exams. She politely thanked me, even as she looked annoyed.

When she spent her evenings in the college auditorium practising for the fest with the college band, I kept looking at her teary-eyed, lurking in the shadows of the empty first-floor gallery. I wanted to strangle every one of those boys.

After a while, I hit upon an idea. Since I had neither her address nor her phone number, so I started sending her letters at the address of the English department, talking about trivial matters from my boring life, just to make her realize that she was the one with whom I wanted to share everything that was going on with me.

She never wrote back or met me in the campus as I requested at the end of every letter. But I still had my hopes high.

❖

Destiny has its own way of kicking you in the balls and shaking you out of your daydream. It happened to me when I was in the final year of my commerce course. Deboleena was also in her final year. We would leave college in a few months.

I had stepped out of the college library that afternoon when I saw Deboleena walking in with her two friends. She saw me and stopped in her tracks.

"Hi, I wanted to have a word with you."

One of her friends rolled her eyes and walked away inside the library. The other stayed back with her.

Deboleena stood at an arm's length and looked into my eyes. Her face glowed from the heat, as the warm afternoon breeze played with her hair. My pulse raced. That was the first time that Deboleena had wanted to talk to me. I silently thanked god and sent up a prayer.

"You need to stop sending me those letters," her words almost whipped me. "You send those letters at the department's

address. The office bearer calls me to the office and hands me those letters, giving me funny looks. Everyone in the office and in my class starts gossiping. You know how it is. You do realize that you are making it very difficult for me, don't you?" She paused for breath.

I opened my mouth, but my words failed me.

"Ask him why he has to write letters to you," the friend said, almost in ridicule, "when we are all in the same campus?"

Deboleena's eyes were fixed on me. "Do you have an answer for her? Why do you have to write letters to me, when we are all in the same campus?" she repeated.

I broke into a sweat. A part of me was dying to scream, "I need to write to you as I hardly get to talk to you in the campus. I don't have your address, or your phone number. But I cannot live without talking to you. I cannot live without sharing with you my little joys and my deep sorrows. I write to you as I want you to realize how much I love you." Then, there was a part of me that saw the anger and the hatred in her eyes, probably a hint of pity too, as she probably thought that I was a fucking psycho.

I decided that the best option for me was silence. The conflict between the two warring halves of me was not resolved. I stood there with my head bowed, not a word escaping my bitter mouth, as boys and girls passed by us, looking at us with curiosity. Any "boy-girl problem" in the campus was fodder for entertainment.

"Do not, I repeat, do not write to me or follow me around in the campus, ever again. I'm warning you." The love of my life turned away and walked briskly towards the library.

Then, she stopped and turned towards me. She walked a few steps towards me and said, "Oh, by the way, you got the spelling of my name wrong in each one of your letters. It's 'Deboleena', spelled with an 'o' and not an 'a'." Having said this, she walked into the library without looking back.

I had not noticed when dark clouds had gathered in the sky. As I stepped out of the library premises, the wind grew strong, and dust started circling skyward. My eyes stung and I knew that I would not be able to hold my tears long enough. That would be quite a scene. The skies, however, took pity on me and opened up. I started running towards the hostel in the rains, tears streaming down my eyes.

But I had still not lost my belief in fairy tales. Deboleena with an 'o' would be mine someday.

9 | A Breakthrough

Kolkata, Present Day

Agni had taken the first sip of the piping hot black coffee when Arya stormed into his office.

"Agni, we have a breakthrough!"

Agni put the coffee mug down and asked Arya, "What do you mean?"

Arya pulled a chair and sat down.

"Let me explain. We got hold of CCTV footages from Paradise. There is a camera that faces the road in front of the hotel. We saw that Ms Mukherjee's BMW left the premises of the hotel at around nine that night. A few minutes later, a black SUV came out from a narrow lane right opposite to the hotel and went in the same direction as Ms Mukherjee's BMW. We made a note of the registration number of the car.

"I looked at camera footages from all the major traffic signals on the way. The SUV was seen following the BMW at safe distance up to New Town. The last footage was from the junction where Ms Mukherjee's car turned right towards her residence. Her car was again followed by the black SUV.

"For the next few hours, there's no trace of the SUV. It comes back on the radar a little after twelve in the night. It can be seen speeding down the empty roads of New Town at anywhere between a hundred and hundred-twenty. It jumped every single red light and was on its way towards Baguiati. The driver almost ran over a woman and hit another car. It was the same SUV that had followed Ms Mukherjee's car from Paradise earlier in the evening. We tallied the registration numbers from the traffic camera footages.

"We checked the registration details of the car. It is registered in the name of a certain Bilal Shaikh in Baguiati. I went to the address. Bilal runs a car rental service. There was no entry in the books about the rental of that particular car on that day. Bilal was initially reluctant to divulge information but came around when I threatened him with immediate arrest on charges of obstruction of justice. It turned out that the car had been hired by a man by the name of Wajid Shamim. He was, apparently, a regular client for Bilal. Wajid was immediately taken into custody. We searched his house and found a gun and a silencer."

"Brilliant!" Agni jumped up from his seat. "Have you found any ID on him? What about his license?"

"He has a driving license. His name, indeed, is Wajid Shamim."

"What about the gun?"

"The gun is not a licenced one. He could not explain satisfactorily why he keeps one. We also found a pair of gloves in his possession. If he had used the gun, he had been cautious. We could not find his fingerprints on the gun."

"Of course!" Agni said. "How can we be sure that it was Wajid who shot Avigyan inside Ms Mukherjee's house that night?"

"I will come to that, Agni. In addition to the traffic camera footages that clearly show the movement of the SUV that day, we have also tracked the location data from the mobile phone we seized from Wajid. It turns out that, he was at the airport in the morning. He then went to the vicinity of Paradise on the Bypass, and stayed there for several hours during the day. He was then found to have driven to New Town. He was there for some time, and then, he started on his way back before he handed over the car at Baguiati and went home. This completely tallies with how the killer might have moved around that night. Also, the gun confiscated from Wajid is a 0.32 calibre. It's the same make that was used to kill Avigyan."

Agni sat up straight. "In that case, this could be the man we are looking for," he said. "We will have to go through his call records from that day."

"We will take care of that, Agni."

Agni seemed to be lost in thought. When he looked up, his eyes had the distant look that Arya was too familiar with. He said, "If Wajid is indeed the killer we are looking for, then Avigyan was being followed from the moment he reached Kolkata. Why?"

He paused briefly, and then muttered to himself with his brows creased, "And then, there is the business of the drug overdose!"

10 | The Right Questions

Agni was busy making notes on the whiteboard about the progress of the case so far. He kept talking with Arya for his audience, as he wrote down facts, his theories and questions that bothered him.

Deboleena Mukherjee was found dead at her residence. She died from an overdose of sedatives, mixed with the wine she had consumed with a companion. An empty bottle of the same drug had been found in the house inside a kitchen cabinet.

She was a widow in her mid-thirties and lived alone in her house in New Town with an attendant Manoj, and a cook Pratima. As Manoj had mentioned, she was not in the habit of bringing friends along, especially during late hours. That night, however, was an exception. She had also informed her servants that she would not have dinner at home.

Her call records showed that she had been in touch with Avigyan before he had arrived in Kolkata, and then, on the day when he was there. They had befriended each other on Facebook a couple of weeks back. They had planned a rendezvous in Paradise where Avigyan had put up. She was seen arriving at Paradise around seven, she spent a couple of hours at the hotel bar with Avigyan and was then seen leaving the hotel with him around nine.

She reached home around ten, when the servants were already retiring for the night. She was last seen alive by Manoj, her Man Friday. He saw her going upstairs with a gentleman. Both the servants heard Ms Mukherjee and her companion talking and laughing upstairs. They heard music playing, like Ms Mukherjee did every night. That was the last anyone saw or heard Ms Mukherjee. The next morning, she was found dead in her room, when Pratima went upstairs to serve them tea.

He looked at the board and murmured while scribbling, "*The only other relative she has in town is an elder brother – Debesh Roy. Her lawyer, Mr Tarun Bakshi, used to visit her frequently. Mr Roy is presently in hospital after he suffered a cardiac arrest on receipt of the news of his sister's death. We've been advised by the doctors not to interrogate him till the time is right. We know that he met his sister that fateful morning, and then called her twenty-seven times on her mobile phone. We will need to figure out why.*"

Agni stopped writing and took a sip of the coffee. He then turned to the board and started writing again.

The other victim – Avigyan Chowdhury. He came down to Kolkata from Mumbai for a*n unknown errand. He meant to stay here just for the night and leave the next day. He had put up in hotel Paradise. Apparently from his phone records, he knew at least two persons in Kolkata – Ms Mukherjee, and another person we are trying to track.*

He got in touch with Ms Mukherjee and the other person after reaching Kolkata. In the evening, he met Ms Mukherjee in the hotel bar, and after a couple of hours, they left in Ms Mukherjee's car.

He was seen in Ms Mukherjee's company inside her house by Manoj. He was heard by Ms Mukherjee's servants. The next day he was found dead inside Ms Mukherjee's house – an overdose of sleeping pills with his wine, as well as a bullet through the skull!

He had consumed the same wine that had killed Ms Mukherjee. Post-mortem reports have reported in his viscera, an overdose of the same drug that killed Ms Mukherjee. He was also shot at very close range in his head by a 0.32 calibre gun.

Agni turned to Arya and said, "By the way, Arya, I have got permission and have reached out to Crime Branch officials in Mumbai to run a check on Avigyan Chowdhury. His house in Mumbai would also be searched.

"Let us now focus our attention on Wajid. We have reasons to believe that he is the killer we are looking for. Camera footages and location data from his phone reveal that he waited near Paradise through the day and when Avigyan left with Ms Mukherjee, he followed him to Ms Mukherjee's house in New Town.

"He entered the house from the backyard. The servants did not see or hear him crossing the lawn, climbing up the rain-pipe and making his way to Ms Mukherjee's room on the first floor, as the doors and windows to the backyard were shut on the ground floor. It was late in the night and they were probably in deep sleep.

"Wajid entered Ms Mukherjee's bedroom through the balcony, unseen. Both Ms Mukherjee and Avigyan had already consumed the drug and were unconscious. Wajid had no way of figuring that out. He shot at Avigyan from close range. He used a silencer, so the gunshot was not heard by the servants sleeping downstairs.

"Wajid retraced his path out of the house and got into his car. He was, naturally, in a hurry and jumped all the signals on the route. This was also picked by the traffic cameras at the junctions. The CCTV footages from Paradise, as well as from the traffic cameras, gave him away. When the police searched his house, he was found to be in possession of a phone, a 0.32 calibre pistol with a silencer and gloves."

Agni paused and started writing pertinent questions:

Who poisoned Ms Mukherjee and Avigyan, and why?
Was only one of them meant to die from the poison, and the other was collateral damage?
What did Ms Mukherjee and Mr Roy talk about that morning, which prompted twenty-seven calls from Mr Roy later in the day?
Why was Avigyan shot but Ms Mukherjee was not?
Why did Avigyan come to Kolkata for a night, and end up dead along with Ms Mukherjee, just two weeks after befriending her on Facebook?
Why had the killer been shadowing Avigyan from the moment he had arrived in the city?
If this was the job of a professional killer, who had hired him and why?

Agni pulled a chair and sat down, looking at the hardly decipherable scribbles on the whiteboard with a sense of achievement. It always made him happy when he managed to crystallize random thoughts, and arrive at concrete questions, whose answers he should chase. The questions got answered, and sometimes new questions got added to the list, as he worked though the case.

He turned towards Arya with a smile, and asked, "Did I miss anything, my friend?"

Arya said, "We've now got details of Wajid's calls over the last three months. He called a number on the night of the murder a little before ten. He's been receiving calls from that number over the last three weeks. And guess what?"

Arya paused for effect, and then went on, "We found that number on Avigyan's mobile as well. That's the person, besides Ms Mukherjee, with whom Avigyan talked a couple of times on the day he was in Kolkata."

11 The Stains

Agni looked at the man sitting across the table. His long locks partially hid his face; the stubble had almost grown into a beard. The barrel-chested man had broad shoulders and his muscles bulged through his fitted T-shirt. There were dark circles around his tired eyes. The last few days had been very difficult for Wajid Shamim.

Agni noticed that the man had a rather peculiar habit. He kept rubbing his t-shirt near his chest and his denim pants around his thighs from time to time, as if to remove stains on his clothes. Agni, however, could see none.

Wajid thought that the man sitting in front of him was very different from the other cops who had interrogated him all these days. This one did not raise his voice or lose his composure, but the piercing look in his eyes was cold and intimidating.

"Why did you kill Avigyan Chowdhury?" asked Agni.

Wajid did not reply.

"I asked you a question, Wajid. It is in your best interest to answer my questions. If you try to act smart now, you will make it more difficult for yourself."

"What proof do you have?" Wajid spoke through clenched teeth.

Agni said, "Wajid, I am not bound to answer your question. But I will still reply, because I want you to realize that you have landed yourself in a mess. Firstly, we have found in your possession a 0.32 calibre gun fitted with a silencer, and a pair of gloves. The victim had been shot by an identical gun. We have collected location data from your phone. You were at the airport in the morning, then followed the victim to Hotel Paradise, then spent the day waiting for him near the hotel, and finally followed him to New Town.

"Your location details reveal that you were at the location of the murder when it happened. Thereafter, you left New Town and started speeding towards Baguiati. You jumped traffic signals, as you were obviously in a hurry. We have CCTV recordings from Paradise and also from traffic cameras that clearly show the number of the car that you were driving that night, and that confirm the pattern of your movements on the day and the night of the murder, as indicated by the location data of your phone.

"Bilal Shaikh has given us a signed statement that says that not only did you hire the SUV from him on the day of the murder, but you have hired cars from him on several occasions in the past. And, here comes the clincher…"

Agni paused for effect and bent forward. Wajid looked into Agni's eyes. His heart skipped a few beats.

"There was a CCTV camera in the house facing the backyard with night vision enabled that recorded you scaling the compound wall and running across the lawn towards the house. You are quite a sprinter, my friend." Agni smiled.

He knew that there was no such camera in Ms Mukherjee's residence. But, this piece of information had the effect of breaking Wajid completely. His shoulders drooped, and he hid his face in his palms.

"Just as I had thought," he whispered to himself, loud enough for Agni to hear, as he shook his head.

"Just as you had thought," Agni repeated after him. "So, Wajid, let's talk. Why did you kill Avigyan? Old scores? Since when had you known him?"

"No," Wajid sat up straight and looked at Agni. "I didn't know him."

"Then, why did you kill him?"

"It was a contract. I was going to be paid the next day."

"That means you are a contract killer." Agni asked, "How did you receive the contract?"

"By phone."

Agni pulled out Wajid's phone that was now in his possession. He scrolled through the call records. He thrust the phone in front of Wajid's eyes and showed him the number Wajid had dialled a little before ten on the night of the murder. Wajid did not save numbers; he memorized them.

"Is this the number?" asked Agni.

"Yes, it is." Wajid nodded.

"Someone you know?"

"No, never worked for…" Wajid hesitated. He was still not sure if the caller had been a man or a woman.

"Him or her?" Agni voiced his doubt as he completed the sentence for Wajid.

"I am not sure," said Wajid.

"What do you mean?" Agni's eyes narrowed.

"The caller used voice modulation. The voice came heavily distorted."

"You called your client that night. Why?"

"I had to make that call as the target had changed his plans. He was supposed to go to Salt Lake alone. I had planned to finish him off on the way. Instead, I saw him leave the hotel with a woman and they went towards New Town," said Wajid as he rubbed the sides of his denim pants again.

There was a knock on the door and Agni turned around. It was Arya. Agni gestured to him to enter the room.

"Agni, we have traced the number from which the call was made to Wajid. The number belongs to a man named Madhav Singh, with an address in Jharkhand. Ranchi, to be precise."

Agni turned towards Wajid and asked, "Does that name ring a bell?"

"Never heard of him," said Wajid.

"Great job, Arya!" Agni turned around. "We need this man. Have you called Ranchi?" Arya nodded in confirmation.

Agni stood up and signalled at the constable to take Wajid away. As Wajid was being taken away, Agni saw him ferociously rubbing the front of his t-shirt.

"Wajid," he called out. Wajid stopped in his tracks and turned around to face Agni.

"Those stains, the ones you are trying to rub off, they will not go away, my friend. They are not on your clothes. You have them on your soul."

12 Wajid Shamim

Wajid Shamim was in his late thirties, but his fitness belied his age. A rigorous workout regime was built into his daily routine and he could run twenty kilometres without feeling breathless. He was a tall man with broad shoulders and enormous hands, which gave him the look of a professional boxer. Years of rigorous exercise had toughened his muscles, and his body showed no sign of sagging. He moved fast and spoke slowly.

For years, he had been serving his Maalik – as he called his prime benefactor – with everything from threatening bureaucrats to getting work done, breaking arms and legs if the situation so demanded and occasionally, taking lives without asking questions.

Wajid had been with Maalik for more than a decade and they had a fantastic working relationship, as none of them believed in investing personal emotions into a job at hand. It was all about achieving goals. They did not celebrate successes, just as there was no remorse if the job failed. Wajid had made it clear to Maalik that he would pick up contracts from others, if the money was good, only if the job did not mean conflicts with Maalik's interests. Maalik had no problem with that.

Settled in his living room with a glass of his favourite Scotch whiskey, Wajid felt relaxed. He had just finished a job for Maalik, and the payment had been received that very morning. He did not have much to do in the next few days. Suddenly, he was snapped out of his reverie as his phone vibrated.

He picked up the phone with his fingers greasy with the deep-fried pakoras and squinted at the screen. The screen flashed an unfamiliar number.

"Hello?" he asked tentatively.

"Hello," the voice at the other end of the line did not sound familiar. "I have a job for you."

Wajid put the glass of whiskey down on the table and sat up straight. The voice sounded odd, in fact, rather eerie. It was a husky voice, and Wajid could not figure out if it was a man or a woman. It also sounded somewhat stifled as if the speaker was deliberately speaking softly, or had his or her mouth covered.

Wajid realized that it was a modulated voice. The speaker was probably using an app on the phone that distorted the voice of the speaker.

"Where did you get my number from?" asked Wajid. The caller did not bother to reply.

Too many questions came rushing to Wajid's mind, but he waited for the caller to continue. Over the years, Wajid had conditioned himself to speak less and listen more – a practice that had always paid off.

As the caller spoke about the job, Wajid kept sipping his drink, letting the instructions sink in slowly.

When the caller had finished and the terms of engagement had been sorted out, Wajid felt happy. The money was more than anything he had earned in recent times. He walked into his air-conditioned bedroom and drifted off to a peaceful sleep.

❖

Wajid shifted uncomfortably on the driver's seat of his SUV. It had been several hours since he had been on that seat, keeping an eye on the hotel across the road. This was not the first time that he had to monitor Hotel Paradise. A lot of his targets put up in that hotel on the Eastern Metropolitan Bypass. The hotel had stopped attracting respectable guests since long.

Wajid turned around and his long hand reached to a thermos flask and a plastic bag behind his seat. He brought out a sandwich, which was cold and soggy, and the smell of mayonnaise and cucumber filled the air inside the car. He poured himself a cup of coffee from the flask. The coffee was lukewarm.

Wajid started his day early. He was near the departure gate of the airport when his target, Avigyan Chowdhury, stepped out not too long after his flight from Mumbai had landed. Wajid pulled up the picture on his phone and verified one more time. Avigyan had apparently booked an app-cab. The cab was taking its time to turn up. Avigyan kept checking his watch impatiently as he made a few calls. Wajid waited inside his car.

When the cab finally picked up Avigyan, Wajid followed the cab, maintaining a safe distance. He had been instructed not to call his mysterious client at any time, unless there was an emergency. Wajid wondered where his mark had decided to put up. His client had no idea. Wajid didn't like to get his hands dirty inside a hotel as there were too many risks.

There would be questions at the reception, if he posed as a visitor and asked for the mark's room number. There would be cameras in the lobby. There was always the possibility, however small, of being noticed by a member of the staff in the elevator, or while walking down the corridor to a room. Wajid knew that one would not forget him easily. In the worst-case scenario of having to do the job inside a hotel, if the mark chose a Hyatt or a JW Marriott, Wajid's job would only get tougher as those hotels have watertight security measures.

Avigyan was expected to be in Kolkata only for one night. He had to be killed before the next day dawned.

❖

Wajid was lucky. Avigyan's cab sped down the Bypass past Hyatt, past JW Marriott, and then ITC Royal Bengal and ITC Sonar, finally stopping at Hotel Paradise.

This was familiar territory for Wajid. Security was slack and the staff had been caught off-guard several times in the past. The hotel survived on people who would rather hide their identities, especially in the afternoons and the evenings when the sleazy bar upstairs was thrown open for perverse pleasures. Nobody would notice an SUV parked opposite the hotel through the day.

Wajid, however, did not want to take chances. He parked his SUV at a safe distance from the road, making sure that he was not too conspicuous, yet he could keep an eye on the hotel from his vantage point. He remembered the instruction of his client:

He would step out in the evening alone and go to Salt Lake. Finish him off then. It's even better if he steps out of the hotel anytime sooner than that. You know what to do.

Wajid turned the air-conditioner on, and played his favourite Atif Aslam songs, slightly reclining in his seat.

❖

It was late in the afternoon now and his mark had not stepped out of the hotel. He saw girls and odd couples going in and out of the hotel at regular intervals all through the afternoon, as he munched on the sandwiches and drank the coffee which he had made for himself before he stepped out in the morning.

Wajid saw the sun go down behind the skyscrapers, painting the sky a dull red. He wondered when his mark would step out of the hotel. His client had not mentioned a time.

It was around seven when Wajid noticed a black BMW roll into the premises. An elegantly dressed woman stepped out. Wajid sat up straight. It was not every day that one saw a woman arrive at Paradise in a BMW! The valet drove her car away.

Around a couple of hours later, Wajid saw the same woman step out of Paradise. This time, she had company – none other than the man Wajid had been waiting for all day! The valet drove her car down and the two of them got in, chatting and laughing. The man got into the driver's seat.

Wajid tied his seatbelt, took a swig of water and started the engine. The BMW went in the direction of Salt Lake and Wajid followed. The BMW crossed the flyover, went past Nicco Park and Sector V, and was headed towards New Town.

Wajid was now at a loss. That was certainly not what he had expected Avigyan to do.

With one hand on the wheel, Wajid dialled the number of his client. The creepy voice answered the call after four rings.

"Why the hell are you calling me?"

"This is an emergency. Mark has changed plans. He is headed towards New Town with a woman."

There was silence at the other end of the line. The BMW was now nearing the mammoth structure of the convention centre in New Town. For a few seconds, Wajid thought that his client had disconnected the call. Then, the ghostly voice was back.

"Don't bother me. You know what to do. He has to be finished off tonight at any cost!"

The call was disconnected.

❖

Wajid slowed down as the BMW ahead had taken a right turn from the main road. It rolled into what looked like a capacious bungalow.

As Wajid drove past, he saw the high wall around the premises, a lawn, and a house that was mostly dark, barring a couple of lighted windows downstairs. He also noticed that there was no other house in the immediate vicinity. He drove on for a few hundred yards and switched his engine off.

Stretching on his seat, he drank from his water bottle, and stepped out. Locking his car, he started walking towards the bungalow. He put his gloves on, and wiping his 0.32 Colt pistol clean, pushed it down the small of his back.

The lights he had earlier seen in the windows downstairs had now been switched off. Wajid walked along the wall to the back of the bungalow and stood at a distance, his eyes fixed on a room upstairs. There was a balcony adjacent to the room and the door leading to the room from the balcony was open. There was a lacy curtain fluttering in the breeze. The room was dimly lit and he could see shadows inside.

Wajid stood rooted to the spot, not taking his eyes off the room even for a second. He reached backward and felt the 0.32 Colt, the silencer already fitted. Wajid waited for close to a couple of hours, till all movements inside the room had stopped. He scaled the wall and then ran across the lawn in a single motion, stooping as much as he could, and reached the back of the house. He had noticed the rain-pipe that went past the balcony. He climbed up the pipe and landed softly on the balcony.

Wajid moved the curtain aside and peeped inside. The man sat lolling on a chair facing the door. His eyes were shut, the shirt was untucked. The blazer was hung over the back of his chair. His legs were stretched forward, and his arms hung on both sides of the chair. The woman was sprawled on the bed. She seemed to be asleep, too. There was a low table between them. There were two empty wine glasses, a bottle of wine and some cashew nuts. Wajid smiled to himself – the idiots had drunk themselves to sleep; no action tonight.

Wajid tiptoed inside the room. Standing at an arm's length from his mark, he pulled out his gun. The barrel kissed the left temple of the man. His jaws clenched, Wajid fired.

The blood splattered as the room was filled with the smell of gunpowder. Wajid was not sure if he had got blood on his clothes. He knew that the doubt would continue to prick his soul, till he reached home, washed his clothes and took a cold shower. He glanced sideways at the woman. No movement; the bitch was in deep sleep.

❖

Wajid followed the same way back to his car. He removed his gloves and wiped the sweat off his forehead. He took a generous gulp of water. His shirt was clammy, sticking to his skin. He turned on the air-conditioner and exhaled deeply.

He had to get away as quickly as possible. There were cameras at the junctions in this part of the city. Was there a camera in the backyard of the house? A lot of those rich people set up security systems in their houses these days.

The roads were empty, and Wajid ignored the red lights as he drove towards Baguiati. He would dispose of the car in Bilal's garage and walk back home, just a tired man who had been working late.

He stepped on the accelerator as he kept rubbing the imaginary stains of blood off his pants.

13 Ill-luck

As Agni walked into the hospital along with Arya, he was greeted by a familiar air of gloom. Nurses and ward boys were ferrying patients in gurneys into and out of the elevators. Relatives waited anxiously in the lobby. Some of them were talking in whispers on phones. Some of them stared blankly at the walls. Some of them were dozing. The air was heavy with the smell of sickness.

Agni took the elevator to the ninth floor and walked towards the cabin where Debesh Roy was being treated. A doctor in a white coat came out of the room as Agni was about to enter.

Agni stopped in his tracks and smiled at the doctor. "Hello doctor, I'm Agni Mitra, ACP, Homicide Department, Kolkata Police. Your patient, Mr Roy, is the elder brother of Deboleena Mukherjee, who was found dead in her residence a few days back. His statement is extremely important for the case. As you are aware, he had suffered a cardiac arrest on receiving the news of his sister's death and was not well enough to be able to talk to us all these days. I got the permission from the hospital today."

"Oh yes," the doctor smiled, "he is doing better now. You can meet him. But, please do make sure that you don't take too long or ask him anything that upsets him."

"I'll try not to ask him anything that is not absolutely essential," assured Agni.

"That would be very nice of you," said the doctor. "I must tell you that while his physical health is getting better, he is deeply traumatized. As it is, he is a patient of acute depression and has been on medication for a fairly long time."

❖

Agni and Arya entered the room, and Agni introduced themselves to Mr Roy. He gestured to a sofa adjacent to his bed. He had a head full of salt-and-pepper hair. It was dishevelled, almost forming a halo around his face, which was chubby and pale, with a few days' stubble. There were bags under his tired eyes. He wore glasses with a thick black frame. The day's newspaper was in his lap.

"How are you doing, Mr Roy?" Agni asked.

"I'm doing better, thank you," Mr Roy forced a dry smile.

"Please accept my condolences, Mr Roy. I understand this must have been quite a shock!"

Mr Roy nodded his head in silence. He then folded the newspaper and put it away. He reclined on his bed and said, "Yes, it was shocking, to say the least. Debo, that's what I called her, was very dear to me. She was about seven years younger. Interestingly, our mother had a cardiac arrest too. She left us when we were very young."

"How did you get the news about Ms Mukherjee's …?" Agni was stopped before he could finish.

"You must have met Manoj. He was Debo's attendant. He called me in the morning," said Mr Roy.

"The house in New Town where Ms Mukherjee lived ..."

Mr Roy did not let Agni finish again. "My father built that house. He passed away six years back. Debo has been living alone in that house with Manoj and Pratima ever since."

"Where did she live earlier?"

"Same house," Mr Roy shifted uncomfortably on the bed. "Debo has been living in that house ever since she returned from Jharkhand. Dad was very fond of her. I have always stayed in South Kolkata, where it is more convenient for me to run my business. My offices are near Ballygunge."

"What exactly do you deal in?" asked Agni.

"Asset Management. We manage portfolios of corporate houses as well as individual investors. We also run a consulting business that provides advisory services for investments, taxes – you know how it works. We have recently launched an online portal as well. You must have heard of Dream Life Asset Management Pvt. Ltd.? That's my company."

"Of course," Agni shrugged. Being consistently callous about monetary matters, he had never heard that name, or the name of any asset management company for that matter.

"You mentioned Jharkhand earlier..." Agni sat up straight. Agni remembered that Wajid Shamim had received instructions for killing Avigyan from a number with an address in Ranchi and mulled over a possible connection.

"Yes," Mr Roy sighed, "that's where we lost Kingshuk in a freak accident."

"Kingshuk – her husband?"

"Yes. He was in Forest Services. He was posted in Netarhat at that time."

Mr Roy paused and looked outside the glass window of his cabin. Adjacent to the hospital was a lake and a boating club, where a small crowd had gathered. The dull grey of the sky was reflected in the water of the lake. The sealed glass window muted out all sounds.

"What exactly happened?" Agni asked, adding, "Of course, if you are comfortable sharing with us."

Mr Roy turned his face away from the window and looked at Agni. "Don't worry about me. I have weathered a lot of storms. Recalling that incident would not make me any worse." He smiled.

"Kingshuk was killed in a shootout, along with a friend," Mr Roy continued, "I can only tell you what we came to know during the trial. The legal proceedings took a long time and we were completely exhausted at the end of it.

"As you know, Mr Mitra, the Maoist movement had taken the state in its grip in those days. There were daily reports of kidnappings, murders, bomb blasts and what not. The police, civilians, bureaucrats – they all had their backs against the wall. No one was safe. No place was safe." Mr Roy paused.

"Were Kingshuk Mukherjee and his friend shot by Maoists?" asked Agni.

"Actually, they were shot by the cops. They were mistaken for Maoists."

"That is the most fantastic story I have ever heard!" Exclaimed Agni, who was now sitting literally at the edge of his seat.

"Yes, Mr Mitra. On the fateful morning, Debo had gone out for a walk near Magnolia Point. She had always regretted that, since it had not been the smartest thing to do under the circumstances. But, what can you do when destiny makes evil designs against you?

"A couple of phone calls had brought Kingshuk and Siddhartha to the same spot. There was a police ambush, out of the blue. Apparently, the police had been tipped off about Maoist movements in that area, at that time of the day. A cop with a history of violent behaviour, landed there with a force and shot them down. By the grace of god, Debo was spared. But, Kingshuk and their friend died on the spot."

"Who was this friend you mentioned?"

"He was a common friend. His name was Siddhartha. They were in the same college," Mr Roy paused briefly, as if contemplating whether he should continue. After a while, he made up his mind and said, "To tell you the truth, Mr Mitra, I never liked that boy. He used to visit us at every available opportunity. It was quite obvious that he was attracted to Debo.

"In fact, I thought he was rather desperate, if you consider the fact that Debo had made her position very clear. Kingshuk and Debo were in love right from the time they were in college and we all knew that they would marry when they felt the time was right. However, there was no stopping our Romeo. In fact, I was very surprised that he continued to be in touch with Kingshuk and Debo even after their marriage, and went down to Netarhat from time to time to meet them. A bad lot!

"Debo was a beautiful and affluent young woman. She often ended up attracting the wrong kind," Mr Roy paused to breathe, and then he said, "You know what, Mr Mitra? I strongly believe that some people simply carry ill luck with them wherever they go. Siddhartha was one such!"

Agni realized that Mr Roy did not have a half-decent opinion about Siddhartha, but he chose not to dwell on the topic.

"Where is Kingshuk's family now?" asked Agni.

"Kingshuk's elder brother lives in Boston. After his death, his parents migrated to the United States to live with their elder son."

"And what about Siddhartha's family? Was he from Kolkata?"

"From somewhere in the suburbs, I don't remember the exact place. Debo went and met his parents after she had returned from Jharkhand. She told me that they were shattered. What else would you expect? Siddhartha was their only child. I was told that they passed away a few years back – both of them, in quick succession.

"I think the passing away of someone you hold very close to your heart breaks you down completely. I can now feel what they must have gone through."

"Did the police find out who had made those calls that morning?"

"No. Never heard about anyone being caught and punished for making those calls."

"What about the cop who shot at Kingshuk?"

"His name was Pratap Jha. I remember he lost his job. He should have been hanged though." Mr Roy's fingers balled up and he punched the bed with his clenched fist. Agni noticed the colour rising to his pale face. The memories of the shocking tragedy had upset him. Outside, the deep blue night was inching like a veil over the glaring red of the sunset.

Agni allowed Mr Roy to regain his composure. He then asked him, "Coming back to the day of Ms Mukherjee's passing away, I was told that you had visited her house in the morning. Did you?"

Mr Roy did not immediately answer. Agni sensed a slight hesitation, camouflaged by an intentional cough, before he spoke again, "Oh yes, yes… I did go over to Debo's house. I did that often, just to check on her. She was a very strong woman, Mr Mitra, and she took pride in her strength. She hardly ever asked anything of me. So, as her brother, it was my duty to make sure that she was looked after." His eyes were brimming with tears. Mr Roy wiped his eyes and cleared his throat, which had choked.

"How did Ms Mukherjee behave that morning? Did you notice anything unusual?"

"Debo was absolutely fine. There was nothing unusual about her that morning."

"Did you speak to her anytime later in the day?"

"I don't exactly remember, Mr Mitra," Mr Roy said, "we might have spoken a few times on the phone, but I don't remember what we talked about. Those were regular calls." He paused for a few seconds and said, "It pains me to think that there won't be any more of those."

Agni stood up, followed by Arya.

"I will take your leave now, Mr Roy. You've been very helpful. I wish you a speedy recovery." Agni smiled.

Mr Roy smiled back and said, "You've been very kind, Mr Mitra. Thank you."

As they stepped out of the room, Agni said almost in whispers, "If there was nothing unusual about Ms Mukherjee that morning, I wonder what prompted those twenty-seven calls. Mr Roy, clearly, is in no mood to tell us!"

14 The Wrong Kind

Agni sat in the balcony, overlooking the traffic on Prince Anwar Shah Road. He held his glass of Glenfiddich in one hand, and the case file, in the other.

This was the time of the evening when everyone was in a rush to go back home to a family, or to a club to wash down the day's fatigue with a few drinks. Ironically, this was also the time when the traffic was at its slowest due to the unmanageable number of vehicles on the road.

Everyone was in a desperate hurry to end the day, and everyone got delayed in the process. Agni was reminded of some hard facts of life. Too much of anything defeated the larger purpose.

One started off doing something, as one enjoyed doing it. Then, one usually ended up doing so much of it that it became yet another chore, and one no longer had fun doing it. It applied not only to creative individuals and businessmen, but also to those like Agni – who enjoyed working through sleepless nights, not paying attention to physical needs, not attaching due importance to monetary returns, seeking only the truth, ready to pay whatever price its pursuit demanded.

At times, Agni wondered if there would come a day when this would become just another job, and an arduous, low-paying one at that. As he took sips of his drink, Agni remembered that, that was the risk Medha would often allude to.

Agni wondered if life would have been different, had he not talked Medha out of the pregnancy in the second year of their marriage, bringing upon himself an overwhelming burden of guilt, that drove him further and further away from her, seeking refuge in the safe territory of his police duties. As the chasm between them grew wider, Medha sought solace in her work that brought her in the company of rich and bored men.

Like those men, Medha tried to substitute the warmth of love and companionship with the sizzle of the forbidden and the sinful. And finally, the inevitable happened. Medha decided to end their marriage. Agni did not stop her. For all his glorious achievements, Agni could not save his wife from the disastrous consequences of the way of life that she had chosen for herself.

Agni remembered that Medha's family had not been supportive when Medha had decided to marry him. Medha's father was a lawyer, and her mother came from one of the most reputed business families of the city. They had reservations about Agni's roots. He was brought up in a small town by his mother, a primary school teacher, after his father had abandoned them and gone away to work in the Mid-East with promises of calling them over, which he never fulfilled, not till the day his wife breathed her last.

Agni saw his mother fight her daily battles to make sure that he had the best possible education that she could afford within her limited means. His father stopped checking on them after a few years, and Agni did not bother to inform him when his mother passed away, leaving him to fend for himself. Medha's parents were confident that, once "the rush of youth and the frenzy of first love wore off", Agni would prove to be a poor match for the city bred, western-educated Medha.

They were also wary of Agni's earnings at the time, paltry by their standards, and the rather bleak prospects of his financial condition matching their expectations anytime soon. They were anxious whether Medha would be able to adjust to a life of calculated monthly spends and cautious shopping, having lived a life of uncompromising luxury in the past.

Most importantly, however, they firmly believed that Agni would have no time for his family, given the profession he was in.

Five years after losing Medha, two-thirds through the bottle of Glenfiddich, Agni decided that he had been no less a man for Medha than any of her other suitors, even with his small-town, single-parent upbringing, long after the "the rush of youth and the frenzy of first love" had worn off. He did concede that his in-laws had been somewhat right about the other two issues. There was not much that he could do about the money and he was not proud about the amount of time he had managed to spend with Medha.

❖

When Medha decided to end the marriage, her parents opposed her decision, not because they had developed any affection for their son-in-law, but simply because, a "divorce" was considered taboo in the family. No one, for generations, had had a failed marriage in the Chatterjee family, the often-miserable status of such marriages notwithstanding, and no one was supposed to make an exception.

Medha, being the free-spirited rebel that she was, did not bother to listen to her parents. When Medha passed away, her parents put the blame squarely on Agni's recklessness and ineptitude in dealing with the case that he was investigating at the time, though Agni was not ruffled by such insinuations. That was also the last that Agni heard from his in-laws. He had no idea where they were now. Not that he cared.

Agni wondered why his mind had meandered to those long-forsaken avenues. Was it the interview with Debesh Roy earlier in the day?

Debo was a beautiful and affluent young woman, Mr Mitra. She often ended up attracting the wrong kind...

Agni wondered if his in-laws had thought the same of him back in the day – the wrong kind.

❖

Agni was so deeply engrossed in his thoughts that the buzz of his phone startled him. Agni put down the glass of whiskey and picked up his phone.

It was a call from Inspector Sudhakar Joshi in Mumbai. Agni had been working with Sudhakar to find out as much about Avigyan Chowdhury as was possible.

"Hello Agni, I hope this is not too late for you," said Sudhakar, the urgency in his voice overshadowing his forced courtesy.

"It's never too late for me," Agni reassured him.

"We've been gathering information about Avigyan Chowdhury. A few interesting details have come up. I thought you should know sooner rather than later."

"That's really nice of you, Sudhakar," said Agni, emptying the glass he was holding.

"For starters, Avigyan had rented a modest single-bedroom flat in Mira Road. He lived alone. We've been to the flat and turned it upside down. Nothing unusual there. We confiscated a laptop. The computer forensics folks will need to break into it—"

"Can you please send it across to Kolkata?" asked Agni.

"Sure, Agni," Sudhakar was only too happy to oblige.

"What did he do for a living? Have you managed to find out?"

"Yes, he ran a casting agency for movies and television serials. It's a shabby little place in Malad, called 'Glamour Unlimited'. Cheap wallpaper peeling off in places, only a handful of workers looking like they couldn't care less, worn out posters of movie stars – you get the picture. We checked out the office, went through files, and talked to a few boys and girls who worked there. The agency doubled up as an acting school and grooming centre for aspiring models and actors."

"Where did the money come from?"

"Mostly from the acting and grooming classes, I believe. No dearth of aspiring actors in our country," Sudhakar chuckled and continued. "I was told that the casting business was not going anywhere. The company is in very bad shape. The handful of boys and girls working there have not been paid for months. Most of the workers have already left."

"Was Avigyan the sole proprietor?"

"Yes, he was. However, we checked company records. It was funded at startup time by a certain Ranjan Chowdhury."

"Also from Mumbai?"

"No, Ranjan Chowdhury has a Kolkata address. Heads a real estate company – Marvel Realtors."

Agni made notes in his pad, as Sudhakar read out Ranjan Chowdhury's address in Kolkata.

"When did the agency start?"

"About eleven years back."

"That's a long time!" exclaimed Agni. "Considering his age, Avigyan must have been in his early to mid-twenties at that time!" Agni made mental calculations and said, "I would not be surprised, if he was just out of college. He must have needed supervision. It's very unlikely that he went solo."

"That does make sense," said Sudhakar. Agni reiterated that he would look forward to receiving the laptop and ended the call.

Keeping the notepad away, Agni kept staring at the darkness. The names "Ranjan Chowdhury" and "Marvel Realtors" sounded familiar.

15 The Warning

"May I come in, sir?" Manoj asked tentatively.

Agni gestured at him to come inside, without looking up from his laptop.

"Sit down," Agni pointed to an empty chair across the table. Arya was already inside the room.

Agni shifted in his seat and fixed his eyes on Manoj.

"Manoj, I have a few questions for you."

Manoj looked sideways at Arya, and then back at Agni. He nodded and said, "I've already told you everything I know."

"That's for me to decide," said Agni.

Manoj wiped the sweat off his forehead.

Agni opened his drawer and pulled out the bottle of sleeping pills that the forensics had found in Ms Mukherjee's kitchen cabinet. He held the bottle up in front of Manoj's dilated eyes and asked, "Does this look familiar?"

"This... this is the bottle of sleeping pills that madam used to take," mumbled Manoj.

"Do you know where she usually kept this?"

"In the kitchen cabinet, along with her other medicines."

"Did she buy this herself?"

"No," Manoj said nervously. "I used to get all her medicines."

"This drug is not sold over the counter without a prescription."

"Yes... yes, sir. I used to take the prescription along."

"Do you have any of those prescriptions with you?"

"Yes, sir. I have them at home. I can show you."

"When did you buy this medicine last?"

Manoj thought for a few seconds and said, "That was three days before madam passed away."

His arms behind his head, Agni looked into Manoj's eyes and said, "You mentioned that Ms Mukherjee's elder brother, Debesh Roy, had come to visit her that morning."

"Yes, sir. He did. He used to visit madam often."

"Did you notice anything unusual that morning?"

Manoj said hesitatingly, "Well, no... I didn't notice anything unusual."

Agni stood up from his seat. He walked around his desk and sat on its edge, facing Manoj. He bent forward, and said, "Manoj, let me warn you. I will give you one more chance to tell me the truth. If, afterwards, I find out from Pratima, or from Mr Roy himself, that you had lied to me, then I will have you arrested on charges of hiding information and obstructing justice. Have I made myself clear?"

Manoj looked away. He wiped the sweat off his face again, and then said in a barely audible voice, "They... they were fighting over something."

"Louder please," Agni said sternly, "I can't hear you."

Manoj cleared his throat and said, "They were arguing over something, which I found very unusual. I had never heard them fight before."

"Why did you say just now that you had observed nothing unusual that morning?"

"I... I thought it was family matter," Manoj stammered. "I am perhaps not supposed to talk about it."

"This is a murder investigation, Manoj," Agni said. "You are supposed to tell me everything!" He went back to his seat and asked, "Did you hear what they were talking about?"

"No, sir. I swear. I was inside my room and I couldn't hear them. But, Pratima told me later that she had gone inside the living room to serve tea. Though they stopped talking as soon as they saw her, she had heard Mr Roy say something to madam just before she walked into the room."

"What did she hear?"

"Mr Roy said to madam, '*I'm warning you one last time. You don't know what you are getting into.*'"

16 The Countdown

Kolkata, 2008

Siddhartha Bose was the only one in the campus who knew about my love for Deboleena. We were in the same class, and Siddhartha had feelings for Deboleena as well. As did half the boys in the college. However, unlike most of the boys, Siddhartha treated me as an equal.

Like me, he came from a lower middle-class family in the outskirts of the city. No flashy shirts, the same trouser worn five days a week only to be washed over the weekend and repeated all through the following week, textbooks borrowed from the library, oily samosas and sweet tea in small plastic cups from the canteen for lunch – Siddhartha and I had a lot in common. I always thought that our humble backgrounds helped us bond.

However, Siddhartha had one enviable quality that catapulted him straight into Deboleena's inner circle. He could sing and how!

Siddhartha had a formidable collection of best singer trophies that he habitually bagged every year in college fests around the city. It was music that brought him close to Deboleena, and the two often sang duets on stage. Needless to say, it was a sore sight for me. Siddhartha made it a point to tease me about it later, with a sense of bravado.

Of course, Deboleena's family, especially her brother Debesh Roy, did not think too highly of Siddhartha. Debesh Roy was an arrogant man who judged Deboleena's male friends only by two criteria – How much money their fathers earned and how much money they were likely to earn themselves. Siddhartha did not score too high on any of those criteria. He himself was aware of his dim career prospects, and had come to terms with the fact that he would have to remain contented with Deboleena's friendship. It would have been ridiculous for him to expect anything more, though, at times, the desperation showed. Still, he was better off than me.

At the very least, he got invited to her birthday party every year, and could drop by at the Roy residence now and then for reasons 'entirely musical'. That definitely gave him bragging rights.

Siddhartha was the only one I stayed in touch with after passing out of college. It was from him that I came to know a year after leaving college that Deboleena had married Kingshuk Mukherjee. It had been common knowledge in the campus that Deboleena and Kingshuk were a couple, although I had chosen to live in self-denial.

Kingshuk came from an affluent business family. He had an elder brother who lived in the United States and he himself had been preparing for a career in Forest Services. Siddhartha had all the information about Kingshuk's family. In fact, he had stayed in touch with Deboleena and Kingshuk even after *college, and now had an invitation to their wedding. I was not sure, if that was something I would have been happy about.*

The news shattered me.

❖

I remember the moment when I heard about Deboleena's marriage on the phone and put the receiver down. My senses went numb and it seemed to me that the world around me was a haze. People around me seemed to be walking in slow motion, I saw their lips move, but not a sound reached my ears. My feet felt heavy and my insides, empty.

I came out of the house and walked into the nearest watering hole. I headed for an empty table in the furthest corner of the room. Though I had never drunk before, it seemed to me that the only way I could cope was to drink my way out of my agony.

The waiter kept serving whiskey on my table, and I kept emptying every glass, even before he had turned his back on me. My grief seemed to have snowballed inside my throat and I was almost choking. I kept wondering if Deboleena remembered the boy who had waited hours outside her examination hall to wish her luck, who had written love letters to her addressed to the department of English, who had roamed the campus with the faint hope of catching just a glimpse of her.

My tears did not stop and before long, I lost count of the number of glasses I had downed.

❖

When I opened my eyes, I saw a clear sky studded with stars. I was lying on a patch of grass.

I tried to lift my head, and it felt heavy. The stench of puke and urine hit my nostrils. I realized that the puke was all over my shirt. I had also pissed my pants. There was a dog hovering around my shoes. I tried to kick it away, but could not gather enough strength. It whimpered and ran a few paces away, only to come back.

There was a bench close by. I managed to climb on to it. My knees hurt as hell, and when I looked down, I saw that they were swollen and bruised, my trousers torn around them. I tried to remember, and blurred images started playing backward in my mind.

Through the fog in my mind, I saw myself falling hard on my knees and being dragged along the ground. I vaguely remembered men holding me by the collar and throwing me out of the bar. I remembered puking on the carpet inside the bar. My hands went to my hip pocket, and I realized that they had taken my wallet. Assholes!

I was inside a park, next to the main road. I could see the coloured specks of the late-night traffic, far away beyond the trees. I imagined men returning in expensive cars from plush offices to warm food and beautiful wives. I wondered what my reality could have been, and what it was. The tears were back.

I looked around. Not a soul in the park, other than the dog sniffing and nibbling on my trousers. I was alone. Alone in clothes drenched in puke, with no money, surrounded by darkness as far as my eyes could see, and nursing a broken heart filled with love that was of no worth to anyone. I felt sick and puked again. And then, the wail made its way up my throat from the depths of my gut. I cried till my lungs ran out of air, and then I cried some more.

When I finally stood up, my legs were wobbly. But, out there, in that dark, cold, deserted park, I kept standing till my feet found their strength back. I had to find my way back to my miserable one-room paying-guest accommodation. I had to sleep off my hangover. I had to sober up for the new day. I had to pick up the scattered pieces of my life. I had to find a job.

When life kicks you in the balls, you swallow your pride. Maybe, I should meet my uncle after all.

Deboleena's marriage gave me a new purpose in life. It was funny that she was not even aware that the countdown had started.

17 | Ranjan Chowdhury

Kolkata, Present Day

A secretary in a sleeveless blouse with thin straps that left a lot of her back bare, and a clingy chiffon saree that had the effect of accentuating her voluptuous figure, opened the door of Ranjan Chowdhury's cabin for Agni. Then, she walked back to her desk, the clicking sound of her pointed heels slowly fading away down the corridor.

No sooner had Agni walked into Mr Chowdhury's office than he knew why the name had sounded familiar. He decided what he would do as soon as he was done with the interview.

Mr Chowdhury sat behind a large desk, smoking from an electronic cigarette. Impeccably dressed in an expensive grey suit, a black shirt and a natty tie, his gel-slick hair was brushed back. He looked up from his MacBook and cast an incisive look at Agni from behind rimless designer glasses.

Agni noticed several miniature models of residential and office complexes around the spacious room. The shelves on the wall to his right were loaded with trophies and shields. Agni's eyes went to a Jamini Roy painting, taking up the entire wall to his left.

Mr Chowdhury blew out a cloud of smoke and almost reading Agni's mind, said with a more-than-subtle hint of pride, "That's an original, in case you are wondering. The market is flooded with fakes, though."

He gestured at Agni to take a seat.

"What would you like to have, Mr Mitra? I am very proud of the filter coffee in my office."

Without waiting for Agni's reply, Mr Chowdhury picked up the receiver of a marble-white phone on his desk and said, "Archana, two cups of coffee."

He then wheeled his chair closer to the table and said, "Let's talk. I'm afraid I don't have a lot of time. As I told you in the morning, I returned from Canada yesterday. My day started with your call and I had to come here to take care of a few urgent matters that could not wait. I need to go back home and get some sleep."

Agni had called Mr Chowdhury in the morning and had come to know that Avigyan was his nephew. Agni cleared his throat and said, "Firstly, my condolences once again, Mr Chowdhury."

Mr Chowdhury took off his glasses and cleaned them with a piece of microfiber cloth. With his eyes fixed on his glasses, he said, "Thank you, Mr Mitra. Avigyan was my nephew. But I looked upon him as the son I never had. I was shocked when you called me this morning. But then, life moves on." He shrugged.

There was an awkward silence in the room for a few minutes. Agni finally said, "His parents—"

Mr Chowdhury did not let Agni finish. He said, "Anjan, my brother, was a loony. He had anger management issues, which everyone in the family had been aware of for years, but no one had done anything about. When we were young, he would bully me at the slightest provocation. I ran away from that mad house as early as I could. Then, it was Avigyan's turn. The poor boy would be traumatised, every time his father decided to discipline him. In any case, it never took much to rub Anjan the wrong way. The rogue was always looking for an excuse to beat people up." Mr Chowdhury looked angry.

Agni wondered if that was caused by the remembrance of his own misery in the hands of a bullying elder brother, or by his love for his deceased nephew. Mr Chowdhury continued, "Avigyan's mother Gayatri had quietly borne the brunt of her husband's unreasonable anger, his foul mood and the thrashings she received from him regularly. A sick family, if you ask me. I made sure that I stayed away from them."

"Where are they now?" asked Agni.

"Oh, the old rogue passed away about..." Mr Chowdhury stopped to count the number of years and then said, "six years back. Gayatri followed a couple of years later."

"So, you were practically Avigyan's only family?"

Mr Chowdhury smiled wryly, "You can look at it that way."

"Did you know that Avigyan would be in Kolkata on that day?" asked Agni, his eyes fixed on Mr Chowdhury. He averted Agni's gaze, and for a split second, Agni observed a crack in Mr Chowdhury's self-assured demeanour.

"No, I did not. He didn't inform me," Mr Chowdhury said.

The conversation was interrupted by Archana walking in. Mr Chowdhury immediately stopped talking and went back to the laptop. The lady laid down on the table, a pot of coffee, two cups, sugar cubes, and a plate loaded with cookies. She poured the coffee into the cups. Straightening up, she smiled sweetly at Agni, cast a quick glance at the boss, who had not bothered to look at her all along. Then she walked away, closing the door behind her.

"I am told that you financed Avigyan's business in Mumbai," said Agni, taking a sip of the excellent coffee.

Mr Chowdhury reclined on his chair, relishing the coffee, and said, "Well, that's a long story, Mr Mitra. I don't know if you are aware of the fact that Avigyan studied in Kolkata. But he didn't stay with me while he was studying. I had offered him accommodation in my house, and I had thought it would be the most natural thing to do.

"But the boy turned my offer down. Said, he would stay in a hostel. Would not take favours from an estranged uncle, I gathered. Though, it really doesn't count as a favour when it comes to family, does it? I agree that I had not been close to them for several years, but, in the end, Avigyan was family.

"Nevertheless, I respected the boy's decision. I did not insist. He stayed in the boys' hostel. He finished his studies. He never was a bright kid, let me tell you. Had taken after his father, I guess. Didn't manage to get a job for a year after he had finished his studies. That was when he finally decided to call on me." Mr Chowdhury smiled smugly, as if he relished his personal victory with his nephew finally seeking his help.

"I believe, it was then that you helped him set up his casting agency and acting school in Mumbai," said Agni. "But, considering that Avigyan had studied commerce and you have a real estate business, he might as well have worked with you. Also, why Mumbai?"

Mr Chowdhury took a puff of his e-cigarette and said, "You didn't hear me, Mr Mitra. As I told you, the boy was no good and I do not compromise on quality when it comes to my own business. I did not have a job for him in my company," Mr Chowdhury paused briefly and said, "There was another reason. My wife ran an acting school and casting agency in Kolkata. Used to groom aspiring actors and models. To be honest, I didn't think much of that business. It was her way of keeping herself busy, while she kept blowing my money.

"But I was an indulgent husband with deep pockets, and never objected to her whims and fancies. She opened an office in Mumbai. Apparently, the prospects there were better, compared to Kolkata. But she wasn't willing to settle in Mumbai for good. Which meant, she needed someone trustworthy to run the business for her in Mumbai. That's when Avigyan came on board. We gave him the job."

Agni thought that the money Mr Chowdhury had invested in the expansion of the business was probably loose change for him. Mr Chowdhury continued, "After a few years, my wife wound up the business in Kolkata. It was just not profitable. Avigyan continued to run the Mumbai office."

Having finished his coffee, Mr Chowdhury looked at his watch. Agni took that as a signal. He stood up. He thanked Mr Chowdhury for his time, said that he would get in touch with him if he needed more information, expressed his condolences once again and stepped out of the cabin.

Turning a bend in the corridor, he could see Archana fiddling with her mobile phone at her desk. When she saw Agni, she stood up. She pushed a strand of hair behind an ear and smiled at him.

"Are you detective Agni Mitra? You solved the Hiya Sen murder case, didn't you?"

Agni stopped in his tracks. He smiled back and said, "Yes, indeed." Agni was getting used to public attention in the wake of the extensive media coverage of his investigation of the murder of Tollywood heartthrob Hiya Sen, who had been brutally raped and murdered a few days after her fairy-tale marriage with the business tycoon, Manav Chauhan.

"I followed that investigation very closely, Mr Mitra. I…I am a big admirer…" she did not finish. Agni saw her blush.

"Oh, thank you," said Agni.

"Are you now investigating Avigyan's murder?" asked Archana, wide-eyed.

"That's right," said Agni.

"Ranjan… Mr Chowdhury told me about it this morning. As you know, it was only yesterday that he returned from Canada. He is very upset and under a lot of stress," Agni did not miss the genuine concern in her voice. He wondered if her relationship with Mr Chowdhury was strictly professional.

"How long have you been working with Mr Chowdhury?" asked Agni.

"About twelve years now," replied Archana with an air of seriousness, realizing that she was helping a murder investigation.

"That's a long time! You must be knowing the family well," said Agni.

"Oh yes, Mr Mitra, I do! Avigyan and Ranjan… I mean, Mr Chowdhury…"

They both heard heavy boots on the corridor. Before long, the portly frame of Mr Chowdhury came into sight, as he turned the bend. Archana cast an alarmed look in his direction and stopped abruptly.

"Isn't my car ready yet? I told you that I want to go back home. I need some rest," Mr Chowdhury almost shouted at Archana.

"Y…yes, sir. Let me call the driver," she went back to the phone.

Mr Chowdhury looked at Agni, not trying to conceal his annoyance, then at Archana, back again at Agni and then said, "Mr Mitra, you are still around. Need a drop?"

"No, I'm fine. Thank you, Mr Chowdhury," Agni smiled and walked towards the door.

After getting into his car, Agni called Arya. He said, "Arya, I met Ranjan Chowdhury just now and I know why the name had sounded familiar. A couple of years back, there was a devastating fire in a slum in the Dhakuria area. Around thirty persons, including women and children, died. There were rumours that a real estate company had hired goons who had tried to evacuate the slum by force, and when the occupants refused to budge, the goons set their houses on fire. I need to know who oversaw the investigation."

Agni paused briefly and said, "The real estate company that was rumoured to be responsible was Marvel Realtors, headed by Ranjan Chowdhury."

18 Glamour Unlimited

Mumbai, 2009

Double infidelity is usually not the best way to start a relationship, but that was how my relationship, if it can indeed be called one, with Shona started. She was married.

As for me, Deboleena was still a sore wound in my heart that had not healed and would never do. I had felt committed to my love for Deboleena for years, and I did not see that changing anytime soon.

But that night, when my eyes landed on Shona, I was almost blinded by her beauty and her sensuousness. Her long, silky almond-hued hair, her black eyes that could penetrate into your soul, her full mouth, her curvaceous body that filled out the evening dress – she looked beautiful. You could hardly tell that she was a few years older than me. I could feel an instant rush of lust coursing through every vein in my body. I could not keep my eyes off her. I watched her from the bar, talking animatedly with her male companion, who had been with her all through the evening. It looked like they were arguing over something, and before long, the guy walked out of the club in long strides.

We were at a party thrown by a producer. Shona knew him and I was working with his casting director on his next project. It was not too often that Glamour Unlimited, the agency which I ran in Mumbai, managed to grab plum projects, or I got invited to parties in upmarket clubs like this one. Therefore, I had stationed myself at the bar. Once the pleasantries had got over, I was busy in making the most of the free booze.

Those were the times when I silently thanked my uncle. He had funded the Mumbai operations of the agency and had put me in charge. Of course, my job had nothing to do with what I had learnt in college, but at the end of the day, I had a job and some money in the bank. The booze and the occasional hookers were bonus!

No sooner had her friend left than I walked up to Shona.

"Is your friend coming back?" I asked her.

"I don't think so," she replied. It did not look like she regretted the fact.

"Would you like another drink?" I asked, noticing her glass was empty.

"Sure," she said.

I walked back to the bar with her and ordered two more drinks. We stood at the bar, making small talk, mostly about work.

"Do you like this?" she asked, her eyes sweeping across the club, "Life on the fast lane. Show business. Glamour."

"I am beginning to like it, I think," I said.

"I've always liked it. I dropped out of college, you know. I wanted to just go out there and 'live'! How could you have the patience to keep studying commerce for three years?"

"I guess, I lacked the courage to go out there and 'live'. Maybe I am a coward," I smiled sheepishly.

"No, you're not a coward, darling. If you were a coward, you wouldn't be here tonight. In a world you know nothing about," Shona laughed, throwing her head back.

My hormones raged inside me. I wanted to grab her and suck her moist, succulent lips hard. I had never experienced such an overwhelming physical desire for any woman before. I wanted to pull her close and feel her body on mine.

I was not sure if Shona saw the lust in my eyes. "I think we should get going. It's getting late," she said.

We left the club and got into Shona's car. She offered to drop me at my flat, which was on the way. We rode the short distance in companionable silence. When we arrived, Shona gently pressed her lips to mine. I could feel the fire in her breath fanning my face. She disengaged and said, "Let me see you off upstairs."

I fumbled with the key to the door of my one-bedroom flat as I struggled to restrain myself any longer. We were barely inside before I pulled Shona towards me, and she caressed my throbbing hardness over my trousers.

"See, you are not a coward. I told you," she giggled and took my upper lip between her lips, then the lower, and then slid her tongue inside my mouth. As our tongues wrestled, we undressed in a frenzy and fell on to the bed. With our mouths sealed in a kiss, Shona yanked down my boxers, and I almost ripped apart her flimsy, soaking panties.

Shona guided me inside herself, and wrapped her legs around me, pushing me closer and deeper with her heels. Thrusting her breasts on to my mouth, Shona built up a rhythm in no time. The room was filled with the smell of sex and our guttural animal cries, as we came together – an indistinguishable lump of naked flesh, slick and hot.

We lay in each other's arms before we were aroused again. This time, I spent hours exploring her body. Every inch. Every nook and crevice. Every spot that I had not explored before, and in return, I was rewarded with pleasure that I had not experienced before.

We made slow, passionate love all night, till light seeped in through the cracks in the heavy curtains that covered my windows.

Shona kissed me on the lips and got off my bed, pulling the sheet along to cover herself. I watched her picking up her clothes from where we had thrown them carelessly last night and making her way to the bathroom from where she emerged fully dressed, ready to leave.

But, a voice inside me told me that we had just started.

❖

Shona and I rode the wings of time as it flew. I could feel my life invigorated by the warmth of what we shared. I could not find a name for it, but Shona was my invitation to life and I grabbed it with both hands.

Every time I came close to her, every time I smelled her, a wave of excitement ran through me. Her exuberance was infectious, and it often made us do the impossible.

Like that one time in a resort away from the din of the city where we spent a weekend, I sat by the pool watching Shona swim back and forth in the middle of the night, drinking straight from a bottle of vodka. When the bottle was two-thirds empty, she invited me into the water and we fucked right there. We fucked all the time. It seemed to me that I was consumed by my lust for Shona. Always hungry for her! Always needing to touch her! Always needing to be inside her!

Soon, I reached a stage where I needed to live our moments of intimacy even when she could not be with me, on those rare occasions when her family took precedence. She was my fix and I needed my release. That was when I hit upon the idea of filming our encounters, to be relished when I was left high and dry.

I wondered if I should do it with her consent. After all, she was a crazy woman. It was unlikely that she would refuse. But then, what if she did? What if the idea scared her, just because there was a husband involved? I realized that there was prudence in being discrete about the whole business.

I went about the job like a pro, and before long, I had a library of home-made porn to jerk off over, when the lead actress was not warming my bed.

Often, late in the night, alone in my room, right after jerking off over one of our videos, I wondered how Shona and Deboleena were different. The answer was not too difficult to find.

Shona made me think of light, of warmth, of passion and of laughter.

When I thought of Deboleena, I could think only of darkness, of sadness, of tears. Of love. And of intense hatred that only true love could breed.

19 | A Bitter Taste

Mumbai, 2009

The curtains of my room were drawn. In the subdued glow of the neon light that trickled into my room from a streetlamp, Shona began to undress in front of me. I lay in bed as she stood in the middle of the room, removing her clothes one after the other, looking into my eyes. I could hear sounds of a typical Mumbai night – cars, motorbikes, loud conversations, boisterous laughter.

Amid all this, Shona stripped down to her undergarments. Her eyes still fixed on mine, she reached back and undid the hook of her bra. Her breasts, firm yet supple, sprang free, the brown nipples already stiff.

I had seen Shona naked before, but that night something felt different. Different because, as she undressed with her eyes locked into mine, it seemed to me that she was challenging me with her nakedness, giving me proof of her trust. I knew that the camera was recording every move she made and that terrified me, as I knew that I was not worthy of her trust.

I wondered if my nervousness showed, if it was very evident that I was not who she perhaps thought I was. Tonight, by undressing the way she was doing, Shona was also getting me naked.

❖

We had just had fantastic sex and Shona was lying with her head next to my heart, her nails drawing circles through the hair on my chest, when she whispered, "I love you."

Her proclamation of love took me by surprise. You see, I did not make too many vows as I trusted myself to keep a vow when I made one. I had made a vow to myself that I would never say those three words to any woman other than Deboleena unless I felt, beyond any reasonable doubt, that I wanted to spend my life with that woman.

To me, love was nothing but pain and grief that we sought, accepted and endured without complaining. It was not about fucking the woman in my arms right now, it was not in the good times I shared with that woman. But, I had the feeling that Shona would not understand any of this.

So, I chose to keep quiet after Shona's whispered declaration of her feelings for me.

"Did you hear me?" Shona asked.

"Yes, I did," I replied and reached for my pack of cigarettes. That was the most honest answer that I could think of at that moment.

After that, there was a fairly long silence, as Shona's fingers stopped drawing circles on my chest. Then, she got off the bed *and pulled the sheet along with her to cover herself up. She went to the bathroom and stayed there for more than fifteen minutes. I assumed that Shona had gone there to cry. I thanked my stars that she had been kind enough to do that quietly, so that I could not hear. I stayed in bed, wondering what I would tell her when she came out, something that would be kind as well as honest.*

When Shona came out of the bathroom, she put on her clothes and came back to bed. I reached out for her but she told me that she was tired and turned the other way to sleep.

❖

Three days later, I was winding up work at the office when I saw an email pop up. It was from Shona.

"Shit!" I muttered and opened it.

The email ran into several hundred words and it was obvious that it had been carefully edited for the right choice of words. It was a meticulous analysis of my pathetic character, which read almost like the clinical notes of a psychiatric patient.

By Shona's analysis, I was a damaged and dysfunctional animal who stood in the way of his own happiness. All I could do was cause pain to others. Never having been in a healthy relationship, I was scared and ran from a relationship, even when it was offered to me on a platter. I took those who loved me for granted, and would probably realize how stupid I was when someday I hit rock bottom, alone, unloved and regretting all the lost opportunities life had sent my way.

Her 'ominous' prediction was followed by a description of the doubts that Shona had had before writing that email, instead of simply calling me and telling me that our no-strings-

attached relationship was over. She had concluded that it was only fair that she explained to me 'in writing' why she, and every other woman on the face of the earth, would find me disgusting unless I changed myself. She went on to say that she was not angry, but sad. She ended the mail saying that she would be happy to meet me so that we could decide if I wanted the relationship badly enough to give it a second chance.

After I reached the bottom of the email, I kept staring at the screen. I closed the mail, shut down the computer, stood up and left the office.

I was not looking forward to a second chance, if it meant that I had to 'fall in love' with Shona.

❖

Even if it had marked the end of a relationship which I now wanted to escape, the mail from Shona had not failed to leave a bitter taste in my mouth.

I knew in my heart that I was guilty of most of the charges that Shona had levied against me. While I had told Shona at the outset that I was looking neither for commitment nor for permanence, Shona perhaps had understood me to mean all of that 'right now' rather than 'never'. I had never felt the need to correct her impression as she was a married woman herself and I had never, in my wildest dreams, foreseen the situation where I found myself now.

I had only wanted a distraction, and a defence against the feelings that had plagued me ever since I had heard about Deboleena's wedding. I had not realized when this casual fling had taken a more serious turn for Shona.

As I was about to enter my flat, my phone beeped. It was a message from my uncle. The old fool had wanted to look at the books of the company, which I knew for a fact did not look good enough. I had been blowing way too much money.

His message went:

Come down to Kolkata immediately. We need to talk.

20 | False Appearances

Kolkata, Present Day

Agni was halfway down his glass of whiskey when he saw Archana Gupta walking towards his table. She looked gorgeous in a pink chiffon saree and a matching sleeveless blouse.

"I'm so sorry, Mr Mitra. There's always so much to take care of at the office."

Agni had started wondering if Archana would turn up at all. He had called her earlier in the day, saying that he wanted to discuss a few things with her about the case. She had sounded as star-struck on the phone as she had when they had talked in person. Archana was not comfortable meeting Agni in the office or anywhere near it. She mentioned how her boss had, the other day, categorically told her not to talk to 'the detective' without his permission. However, this was one order she was happy to disobey, as she considered herself lucky to be of any help to "someone like ACP Agni Mitra".

Agni had said that he was flattered. Then, Archana had suggested that they could meet somewhere outside the office. Agni had not missed the cue and had offered to meet her at The Big Ben. Agni was a regular there. The place was not very far from Archana's office either.

"You don't look like you've had a long day at work," Agni said with a smile as Archana sat across the table, her face radiant, her eyes wide in the same schoolgirl-like wonder as the other day, her skin glowing.

"Oh, thank you Mr Mitra," said Archana, as her cheeks turned a shade of pink.

"What would you like to drink?" Agni asked.

"Red wine would be fine."

Agni turned to the waiter, who suggested a Merlot. Archana agreed and the waiter was gone.

"I'm so sorry for the trouble, Mr Mitra." Archana looked apologetic and said, "But Ranjan… Mr Chowdhury – was very angry with me the other day. I did tell him that we were just making small talk. That I had asked you about your cases. But he would not listen. Told me to stay away from you."

Agni smiled and took a sip of his whiskey. "Well, it's not a trouble at all. This is where you would usually find me on that odd evening when I have some time for myself. And I have to say, you can be quite a rebel!"

Archana laughed, throwing her head back, and said, "You can be very charming, Mr Mitra."

"Thanks, Ms Gupta…"

"Please call me Archana," she interrupted.

"It's interesting that you find me charming. Most women find me vulnerable. I probably appeal to their maternal instincts."

Archana took a sip of the wine, which the waiter had served in the meanwhile. She reflected for a few seconds on what Agni had just said. Then she said, "That may be because when they see you, they remember your pain and anger, that was caught on cameras when your wife..."

Agni raised a hand and stopped her. "I try not to remember," he said.

For a few fleeting seconds, Agni remembered Priyanshi Basu, whom he had met a few years back. While Agni tried to keep emotions at bay when he plunged headlong into an investigation, on that occasion, Agni and Priyanshi bonded over their emotional crises caused by the same serial killer. The perpetrator was captured, Priyanshi went back to her job, and life moved on. The two of them had been friends ever since, Priyanshi seeking Agni's suggestion every time she found herself at the crossroads of life, and Agni often finding solace in simply talking to her and taking a load off his chest. Otherwise fiercely protective about his emotional space, Priyanshi was the only one with whom Agni let his guard down in moments of weakness and vulnerability. Probably, the darkness that Agni surrounded himself with, owing to his profession, made it more difficult for him to move on.

Agni was quiet, as he finished his whiskey. Seeing him momentarily disoriented, Archana put her glass down. She moved closer towards Agni over the table and said, "I'm so sorry, Mr Mitra. I shouldn't have brought up the tragedy."

"It's alright," Agni said reassuringly. "I'm trying very hard to stop living in the past."

"Me, too," the smile was back on Archana's full, crimson lips. "There comes a time when you need to confront the reality and move on. We often end up damaging ourselves by holding on to our past."

Agni wondered what she was referring to. A bitter memory? Unfulfilled dreams? Or a relationship that had not turned out the way it was meant to? He gave her the time to regain her composure. He also noticed that she was more than halfway down her glass of wine.

"You wanted to discuss the case," Archana tried to sound professional, but did not quite make it.

"Yes, I wanted to know a bit more about the Chowdhurys, considering the fact that you have been working with Mr Chowdhury for twelve years. You are probably the one who can be trusted to share an outsider's view."

Archana sat up straight, pushed a few strands of hair behind an ear, and tried to look serious. She was more used to taking orders and it was not every day that someone met her over drinks and asked for her opinion on a certain matter. She also wondered for a fleeting second if that was the only reason why she was there at that moment with the handsome cop in front of her – a thought that she did not allow to dwell on her mind for long. She wondered why she was thinking that way. Was it the wine?

"I was told that Avigyan had not informed Mr Chowdhury that he would be in Kolkata," said Agni. "Why do you think he didn't?"

The waiter had turned up to refill their glasses. When he departed, Archana smiled and said, "Is that what Ranjan told you?"

Agni noticed that she had not bothered to correct herself with a more formal way of referring to her boss. The wine was already talking.

"The fact is, Avigyan had not met Ranjan for years," said Archana, taking a generous gulp.

Agni sat up straight, the information taking him by surprise. He asked, "Do you know why?"

"They had not spoken to each other for years. Since the showdown they had in the office."

"When was that?"

Archana thought for a few seconds and said, "Must be about eleven years back. I was about a year into my job."

"I do understand that it was a long time back, but do you happen to remember what happened?"

"I remember very clearly, Mr Mitra. As you know, Ranjan had financed his wife's business in Kolkata. She used to run an acting school and a casting agency. She had also expanded her business to Mumbai and Avigyan had been asked to take charge. The business was not doing well.

"Ranjan had been nice enough not to make an issue out of that. What pissed him off was the fact that there were serious irregularities in the books. Avigyan was throwing Ranjan's money all around. He was living it up in Mumbai – booze, girls. Know what I mean?"

Agni nodded.

Archana continued, "When Avigyan met Ranjan in the office, all hell broke loose. Ranjan said that he would not pay a penny more. Avigyan was extremely disrespectful and started shouting at his uncle. I was shocked. I remember wondering if Avigyan was drunk!"

"That was the last time you had seen them talking?"

"Yes. I know they never spoke to each other after that incident. After some time, Ranjan's wife packed up her business in Kolkata. Avigyan continued to run the agency in Mumbai, but Ranjan had stopped financing it."

"How did Avigyan manage? Any idea? Anything you heard?"

"I'm not sure. There were all kinds of rumours. People even suggested that Avigyan was running a sex racket in the guise of that agency. To be honest with you, I had always found the boy quite disgusting! Always trying to take the shortcut to success, money, comfort. Always trying to milk his uncle for every single penny without any gratitude."

Agni nodded.

"How's Mr Chowdhury's family otherwise? I thought he's very indulgent towards his wife. It seems he's a happily married man."

Archana took a while to respond. She kept looking at the table, and then finished the wine in a long gulp.

"I wouldn't say that Ranjan is very lucky that way, either."

Agni bent forward, and asked, "Really?" He gestured at the waiter to fill their glasses.

Archana leaned back in her chair, her breasts heaving under the thin veneer of the saree, in apparent excitement. "You know, Mr Mitra," she said, "Ranjan married late. His wife, Shivangi, is several years younger. I haven't figured out in all these years, what keeps them going. They belong to different eras, to different worlds, if you ask me. They have nothing in common.

"Be it their tastes in food, in music, in movies, in the ways they live their lives. Maybe it's only the money. They do a fine job of hiding their differences, and coming across as a loving couple, though. If there is one lesson that I have learnt just by observing them, it is that one should never be fooled by appearances." There was already a hint of a slur in Archana's speech.

Agni was still hunched over the table. He realized that, for some reason, this was a sensitive topic for Archana. His question had got her restless. He asked, "What's Mr Chowdhury's wife like?"

"To put it simply, she's just the kind of woman I hate. She has never had to work hard. She has been living off Ranjan's money for years. In fact, that's probably the only reason she's with Ranjan. She runs an NGO in Kolkata. It goes by the name of Hope Foundation. It works for children from the red-light areas of the city. Before that, she worked in Ranjan's office for some time, and then gave up the job to start Glamour Unlimited, the agency we talked about.

"Instead of being grateful, she fights with Ranjan every other day. But Ranjan continues to put up with all that shit! I don't know if that's what happens when you've stayed with someone for years. I don't know if that's what marriage does to you. There's no love, there's no passion. It boils down to 'being around' that person, 'taking care' of that person, 'not upsetting the status quo'," Archana kept drawing quotes in the air with her fingers as she spoke, leading Agni to wonder if those were words that Ranjan Chowdhury had actually used while describing to her his relationship with his wife.

Archana paused briefly and drank her wine. Then, she continued, "I sometimes wonder if Ranjan has actually developed paternal instincts for Shivangi. Because, he kept himself deprived of what could have been a beautiful life, a life full of love and happiness. He had no value for the love that was his for the taking. He could not bring himself to keep the promises he had made to me. I....I remained the other woman." Archana smiled sarcastically. Agni saw her eyes had welled up.

Archana sniffled and reached inside her purse, pulling out a handkerchief. She dabbed it on the corners of her eyes and looked at Agni. With a forced smile, she said, "I'm sorry. Too much of the wine, I guess."

Agni said, "Life's a bitch, isn't it? Like you said, sometimes it's better to confront reality and move on. We damage ourselves by holding on to the past."

Archana nodded, and throwing caution to the wind, reached for her glass of wine. Taking a sip, she said, "Talking of Shivangi, I need to tell you something. This was three weeks before Avigyan's murder. Shivangi came down to the office and went straight down to Ranjan's chamber. I was passing by Ranjan's room on an errand, when I heard them yelling at each other. I must confess, I shamelessly eavesdropped." Archana paused and winked.

"What did you hear?" Agni was on the edge of his seat.

"I'm telling you only because this might be of help. I heard Shivangi saying that she was not asking for money for herself. Instead, she was conveying Avigyan's message. Avigyan had asked for money because he was planning to invest in a new business. He had threatened that if Ranjan did not budge from his stand, then he would go to the police and tell them everything he knew about the fire in the slum."

Agni shifted in his seat. "Do you think he meant the fire in the slum at Dhakuria?"

"Y...yes, that was what I thought as well," said Archana. She looked at her watch and Agni could sense a sudden discomfort in Archana's demeanour, despite her drunken state. She had probably realized that she had divulged more information than she should have. Agni gestured to the waiter that they were ready to leave.

"That's very interesting, Archana. Thanks for sharing this with me."

She smiled warmly, a strand of her hair across her face. As they walked out of The Big Ben, a cold breeze greeted them.

Archana tottered unsteadily on her pointed heels. Agni opened the door of his car and she slid inside.

Agni shut the door and walked around to the driver's seat. He turned the engine on, and then the air-conditioner. Archana leaned back, turned towards Agni, and smiled.

"Thanks for the lovely evening," she said.

"The pleasure was all mine, Archana," Agni replied, "and thanks for all the information."

There was an SUV parked on the side of the road opposite to the hotel. After Agni's car had gone out of sight, the man in the driver's seat picked up his phone.

"Sir, she was with the detective. They left just now," he said.

21 Money Matters

Agni looked at his watch as he stood in front of the imposing compound wall. It was close to nine in the night. That was the time Advocate Tarun Bakshi had said would be best for the meeting.

The roads in Salt Lake were empty at that time of the night, with the few odd private cars speeding up and down occasionally. This was one of the few places in the city where one could still breathe in some fresh air.

The watchman opened the gate and Agni walked down the gravelled path that went right through the impeccably maintained lawn up to the house of Deboleena Mukherjee's lawyer. The trees that lined the compound wall looked like patches of dark ink against the night sky. There was a dog barking somewhere in the distance. That was pretty much the only sound that reached Agni's ears.

Advocate Bakshi lived alone in that house. The sitting room was on the ground floor where the ace lawyer met his clients. There was a library at the other end of the room with bookcases stacked with legal tomes reaching up to the roof. The bedrooms were upstairs.

When Agni walked in, the lawyer was already in the sitting room, smoking his cigar.

He stood up and extended his hand to Agni, "Welcome Mr Mitra. You are on time!"

Agni shook his hand and said, "Thanks, Mr Bakshi. When you manage to find an hour for me from your busy schedule, I better make good use of every available second." The two men laughed.

The lawyer offered Agni coffee which he politely declined. He then asked Agni, "How can I help you, Mr Mitra?"

"As you may be aware, I am investigating the murder of Ms Deboleena Mukherjee, who, I am told, was your client."

"Yes, indeed she was. I was not aware, however, that you are in charge of the investigation. It makes me feel confident that we will soon get to the bottom of this horrible incident. I am frustrated with the way the newspapers and the television channels are scandalizing her death. Dragging in that man who was also found dead in her bedroom. Cooking up all kinds of theories. I don't even know who Avigyan Chowdhury was. Just the insinuation by the media that Deboleena had a clandestine affair with him is absolutely horrendous! Everyone seems to have an expert opinion on the matter!"

"Oh yes, death makes for good business," Agni said with a smirk.

"It does, Mr Mitra," said Mr Bakshi with a sigh. He let out a cloud of smoke and said, "What does it do to someone like you? Someone who sees death from such close quarters every other day and then, has to deal with it, analyse it with clinical precision without letting an iota of emotion get in the way?"

Agni smiled and said, "You ask a pertinent question. I have reflected on this on a number of occasions myself. I end up a little bit damaged every time I engage myself with the investigation of another murder. Unfortunately, there are inevitably more depressing stories and human frailties behind these crimes than what your average thriller story would tell you.

"In my early days, I used to consider myself a knight in shining armour, entrusted with the duty of dispensing justice to mankind. Now, after all these years in the force, I consider myself more of a garbage collector. You see, Mr Bakshi, murderers are usually damaged, vulnerable persons and it is often not very difficult to identify the reasons why they did what they did. And when you finally find them, you feel frustrated. Because they not only screwed up their own lives, but ended up dragging others down the dark tunnel along with themselves."

"That's an interesting way of looking at murders and murderers," said Mr Bakshi. "Let's now talk business."

Agni cleared his throat and said, "By the way, Mr Bakshi, on your point about Ms Mukherjee's relationship with Avigyan, we have managed to find out that they had known each other for some time. They became friends on Facebook a couple of weeks before their death. In fact, they had spoken to each other on the phone on a couple of occasions before Avigyan came down to Kolkata. These findings, of course, do not automatically imply that they were having an affair."

"I see," Mr Bakshi said reflectively. "Of course, I was not privy to Deboleena's personal matters. Tell me, Mr Mitra, how can I help you?"

"Like you said, I hope we do get to the bottom of this quickly," Agni smiled. "I met Mr Debesh Roy, Ms Mukherjee's elder brother, but I still wanted to ask you a few questions. I am sure you are better placed to offer me an outsider's perspective of the family than anyone else I can think of at the moment. I am aware, of course, that you may be constrained by confidentiality agreements with your client, so I don't intend to put you in a spot. Please feel free to let me know if you cannot answer a question, and I will not insist."

"Mr Mitra, that's very kind of you. Let me put it this way. I've dealt with some of your colleagues, who have been less understanding." Mr Bakshi smiled.

"I understand that the house Ms Mukherjee had been living in belonged to her father?"

"That's right. Dwarka – Dwarkanath Roy used to be my client, as well."

"I believe Ms Mukherjee moved into the house after her return from Ranchi."

"Yes. That was a distressing time for the family. Her husband, Kingshuk, was a forest officer in Jharkhand. Deboleena used to teach music in a local school there. Maoist activities were at their peak in Jharkhand at the time. Kingshuk was killed in a shootout. There was a misunderstanding. Can you imagine, the police took him for a Maoist activist? I was told that there was also a friend who had been shot down. She returned to Kolkata and moved in with her father. Dwarka had built the house in New Town around that time. Debesh never stayed in that house. He runs an asset management business. Lives in Tollygunge," said Mr Bakshi, and then added somewhat nonchalantly, "I heard he suffered a heart attack."

"Yes, he is still in the hospital. I met him a few days back. I was told that he had been suffering from chronic depression."

Mr Bakshi thought for a while and said, "Well, Debesh has always been a bit of a rebel. Dwarka ran Life Pharmaceuticals. He had inherited the business from his father and it was a fairly successful enterprise. Debesh worked for a couple of years with Dwarka and then decided to start his own business. He left the house as well, saying he wanted to live closer to where he had set up his office. Life Pharmaceuticals ran into rough weather when Dwarka could no longer lead from the front, closing down finally after Dwarka's death. Dwarka, however, had made a lot of money from the business. On the other hand, Debesh's business never quite took off. I believe he is still struggling. I have also heard that not everything is going great on the family front as well. I am not surprised he suffers from depression.

"Dwarka was not pleased with his son's decision to abandon the family business and he blamed his son's lack of interest for the ultimate collapse of the business. In his will, he transferred the house and most of his money to Deboleena. I am not sure if Debesh took his father's decision too kindly."

Agni nodded and asked, "How was the relationship between the siblings? I thought Mr Roy was quite protective and affectionate towards his sister, notwithstanding the financial arrangements in the family that you just mentioned. In fact, he looked quite shattered when I met him."

Mr Bakshi smiled wryly and said, "To be honest with you Mr Mitra, I do not interact with Debesh a lot. So, I am not the best person to comment on his feelings for his sister."

"Mr Bakshi, now that Ms Mukherjee is no more, what happens to the property?" asked Agni.

The lawyer said, "Well, Deboleena never made a will. She did not marry again after Kingshuk's demise. She never had a child. Under these circumstances, the property will automatically pass on to the next of kin – in this case, her brother, Debesh."

"I thought as much", said Agni. After a brief pause, he said, "That would come as a breather for him, considering the state of his business, wouldn't it?"

"It would... it certainly would," said the lawyer, taking a long drag of the cigar. "There is a lot of money out there!"

22 Maalik

Agni zoomed in on the picture of the woman on his mobile screen. Shivangi Chowdhury looked several years younger than her husband. An oval face with hair parted in the middle, wheatish complexion, a broad smile that for some reason did not reach her somewhat melancholy eyes, her head tilted slightly upwards, possibly in an effort to look confident. She was in a sequinned black saree and a matching sleeveless blouse, with no jewellery around her slender neck.

Shivangi Chowdhury was an attractive woman, no doubt!

The picture was from a charity event organized a month back by her NGO Hope Foundation, which had been attended by the mayor of Kolkata. The event had been covered in all leading newspapers and television channels. The links to those reports were among the first that had been thrown up when Agni had googled her name.

As Agni scrolled down, he saw reports on more events organized by her NGO. In some, she was seen distributing clothes and books to children in the red-light areas of Sonagachi and

Kalighat. In some, she was seen in makeshift schools for those children. In one of the pictures, she was accompanied by Ranjan Chowdhury. Some local news portals had also interviewed Shivangi a few times. Agni looked at some of the videos.

Interestingly, there was no mention of Glamour Unlimited in any of the recent links. On the third and last page of the search results, Agni saw that the last two links were about a talent search event she had conducted in Kolkata for Glamour Unlimited. The reports dated back to 2009. Agni realized, that was around the time when Shivangi had decided to branch out to Mumbai.

Agni was interrupted in his thoughts, as Arya walked in. There was another man in uniform who followed Arya into the room.

"Meet Inspector Samaddar," Arya said. "He was in charge of the investigation of the slum fire in Dhakuria."

Agni stood up and extended his hand.

"Deepak Samaddar," the officer said with a smile and shook Agni's hand. "I follow your investigations closely. Consider me a fan."

Agni laughed. "Deepak, you are too kind. As you must be aware, I am investigating the murder of Avigyan Chowdhury. He was the nephew of Ranjan Chowdhury, who heads Marvel Realtors. The name had sounded familiar to me the day I had heard it and when I saw him, I remembered the face from the news reports. Marvel Realtors' name had come up in connection with the slum fire incident in Dhakuria. I wanted to find out more about the incident. When exactly did the accident happen?" asked Agni.

"That was two years back," Deepak said and smiled dryly. "It's interesting that you call it an *accident*. That's what I had to call it in my report too – an accident caused by a gas cylinder exploding. It was a congested slum, houses breathing on one another. The fire spread within minutes. Everyone was happy with that report. The file was closed. For good!"

Agni could hear the hurt in Deepak's voice, and he bent forward. "So, are you suggesting that there was truth in the rumours about Marvel Realtors?"

Deepak looked into Agni's eyes. "Those were not rumours. Everyone knows it was Marvel's doing. They needed the land to build a shopping mall. Their goons had ordered the slum dwellers to vacate the land." Deepak paused and took a sip of the tea that had been served.

He then continued, "There was a social activist by the name of Ankita Guha, who had taken up the cause of the slum dwellers. In fact, she moved to the area and started living in a one-room house. She spoke to the angry, helpless people, and tried to put up an organized fight against Ranjan Chowdhury. She got some of the boys together and went to the office of Marvel Realtors. Mr Chowdhury did not meet her. Instead, she was humiliated and thrown out of the office. What Ankita had not realized was that Mr Chowdhury had very powerful friends. He walked the corridors of power in the state.

"In our country, it does not take too long for anything to take on political colours. The civic polls were near. The Opposition sniffed an opportunity and jumped into the bandwagon. They started holding street meetings in the area. They got Ankita on the stage and were even willing to offer her a ticket. However, Ankita declined. They tried to convince her that she would never succeed in her fight without political backing. She decided that, if she needed political clout, she would contest the elections independently with the support of the Opposition, but not join any political party.

"But the politicization of the issue actually worsened matters. Almost overnight, it was not just Marvel Realtors, but the political machinery that Ankita was up against. She started receiving threats, goons started turning up at her door at odd hours."

"How do you know all this?" asked Agni.

"She got in touch with me about two weeks before the fire. I heard her story. When she spoke, I could sense the genuine concern she had for the people in the slum. I could see that she was sad for them, and that she was scared. She needed protection, and she requested me to help her. There was an earnestness in her voice I will never forget. There was a sense of urgency. She knew that time was running out and she needed my help. Not just for herself, but for all those people who had started relying on her. Those who looked up to her, those who woke up every morning with the hope that she would get them out of the mess."

Agni kept watching Deepak. He could feel the resentment in his voice. He knew how it felt.

Deepak said, "I put together a team and planned for her protection immediately. I also wanted to protect the people in the slum. But all my efforts were squashed in no time. I was not allowed to provide any security cover to Ankita. The next night, when she was returning to her rented flat near the slum, she was run over by a truck. They made sure that the news of Ankita's death did not make headlines. Did you even know that someone called Ankita had existed? That she had fought for the slum?"

Deepak paused. No one spoke. There was an eerie silence in the room. Unravelling before Agni's eyes was another instance of the eternal battle between the State and the Soul that every policeman the world over went through. The State had its own priorities; the Soul had its own principles. And at times, a policeman had to sell his Soul to the State just to earn his daily bread.

"Did you investigate Ankita's death?" Agni asked after a few seconds.

"What do you think? It ended up being a routine investigation, recorded as just another hit-and-run case. Like the dozens that happen across the city every day."

"What happened next?"

"The slum was burnt down. The goons came in one night with torches and set the houses on fire. Women, children, the aged who could not run for their lives – they were roasted alive.

"But we had orders not to call out Marvel. Not to talk about the unholy nexus Mr Chowdhury has with those in power. We had to call it an accident. A gas cylinder had caused the disaster. Those who were burnt alive were the ones to blame for their callousness. What if the fire had spread beyond the slum? What if it had gutted the houses of the rich, who lived next to the slums? Those were the more important questions. But, do you know what hurts the most? The fact that I could not save Ankita. I could not get her the justice she had come looking for."

Agni nodded and asked, "Did you speak to anyone from Mr Chowdhury's family?"

"No! No one from Mr Chowdhury's office or his family was willing to cooperate. In any case, we received orders to close the investigation. If you don't mind, why do you ask? I'm curious."

"Well, I have information that someone in Mr Chowdhury's family was blackmailing him over the slum-fire incident."

"Really?" Deepak looked surprised.

Agni nodded and asked, "You said that the goons had come to the slum that night with torches. There must have been several eye-witnesses."

"Many, actually! They were also willing to testify. But they were silenced. Threats, bribes, you know how it works."

"Could you track the goons down?"

"Yes. It wasn't very difficult, actually. They had been coming down to the slum frequently, threatening Ankita and the inhabitants of the slum. They were hired by a notorious criminal, who works for Mr Chowdhury. I have the hunch that the scoundrel was also responsible for Ankita's murder."

"You have his name?"

"I do. I gathered evidence of his connection with Mr Chowdhury – that was before my bosses received orders to pull the plug on the case. He calls Mr Chowdhury 'Maalik'. That's a code name. The bastard thinks he can get away with murder just because he has Mr Chowdhury's blessings.

"His name is Wajid Shamim."

23 Madhav Singh

Arya stayed back in the room after Deepak had left.

"Agni, I have news from Ranchi. You will remember that the number from which Wajid had been receiving calls in a modulated voice was tracked to a person named Madhav Singh in Ranchi."

"Of course, I do. That was the number Wajid called that night when he was following Avigyan and Ms Mukherjee to her house in New Town. That number was also found in Avigyan's call records on the day he was in Kolkata. Have they managed to find him?"

"It turns out that Madhav Singh is dead," said Arya.

"What?" Agni screamed in shock.

"Yes. Madhav Singh died about three years back. Jharkhand police tracked down his family. And this is where it gets very interesting," Arya said. "The family is not even aware of that number! The connection was activated a little more than two weeks before the murder of Avigyan. However, the police gathered valuable information from the family about Madhav.

He used to work in a company in Kolkata as a driver. The family has the contact number of his former employer. And guess which company he worked for?"

"I'm all ears, my friend," said Agni, his excitement palpable.

"Madhav was one of the drivers who worked for Ranjan Chowdhury's company Marvel Realtors. Three years back, Madhav came down to visit his family in Ranchi and died of dengue. When Mr Chowdhury came to know that Madhav had died, he called his family in Ranchi, expressed his condolences and sent them money. It seems that Madhav used to be one of Mr Chowdhury's favourite chauffeurs. The family was all praise for Mr Chowdhury's kindness and magnanimity.

"Now the question is, how could a new phone connection for Madhav Singh surface three years after his death?" Arya looked confused. "That's the question that's also bothering Jharkhand police."

Agni was silent. He kept pacing up and down the room. He stopped suddenly, and when he turned towards Arya, his eyes shone.

"Yes, this has to be it!" Agni exclaimed, "there can be no other explanation!"

"And what's the explanation?"

"Arya, how difficult would it be for you to apply for a phone connection in someone else's name if you have a photograph and an identity proof of that person?"

"Fairly easy, but—" Arya was about to say something when Agni interrupted him.

"If that person happens to be driving a company car, then chances are that the office would, in any case, have collected his photo and an identity proof when he started working, as a security measure."

"Well, of course!"

"That means Wajid Shamim received the contract for killing Avigyan from a number that was purposely issued in the name of a dead person, who could not be traced."

"I would say this puts Ranjan Chowdhury in a very sticky situation," Arya said. "We know that he was cross with his nephew as there were financial irregularities in the business he was running in Mumbai. Avigyan was fleecing his uncle for all the money he needed for his extravagant lifestyle in Mumbai.

"The last nail in the coffin was the blackmail threat. His wife informed Mr Chowdhury that Avigyan had threatened to expose his involvement in the slum fire incident. The rumours would have been proved right and Mr Chowdhury could not afford to take the risk. He knew that, if an exposé came from the family, the media would pounce on it and fan public protests which, even his friends in power, might not have been able to ignore and continue to patronise him. Therefore, Avigyan had to be silenced."

24 Discrepancies

Shivangi Chowdhury dabbed her face with a wet tissue and fanned herself with a hand in an exaggerated fashion, suggesting that she found the room very uncomfortable. She had her hair tied back in a bun, and wore a white tee paired with blue denim pants. Her shades rested on the neckline of her tee, revealing a hint of cleavage.

Agni pushed towards her the glass of water that had been placed on the table a while back. Shivangi emptied half of the glass and laid it down on the table, using the tissue once again on the edges of her coloured lips.

"Ms Chowdhury, where were you the day Avigyan was murdered?" asked Agni.

"I was in Kolkata. The annual event of Hope Foundation, my NGO, is coming up in a few days, and we've been busy with preparations for several weeks now. There are cultural programmes where boys and girls from the red-light areas of the city participate. We organize exhibitions of handicrafts made by these children. We hand out cheques worth several lakhs of rupees to schools and welfare organizations. The mayor usually turns up to encourage us. We also have a number of political leaders and celebrities from the entertainment business supporting us. The coordination and the arrangements can be a nightmare, as you can imagine!"

Agni wondered if the mention of the political backing was deliberate. He said, "Of course, I have been reading about the great work you are doing. I saw reports of these events from past years. I also watched some of your interviews."

"You did?" Shivangi asked, her eyes getting wider. She smiled and pushed a strand of hair behind her ear.

"How did you come to know about Avigyan's death?" asked Agni.

"I was with Ranjan when he got the call the next morning."

"I see. When was the last time you met Avigyan?"

Shivangi thought for a few seconds, and said, "I'll be honest with you. I don't remember exactly. Avigyan had not been in touch with us for a very long time."

Agni asked, "But, the agency he ran in Mumbai had been funded by your husband?"

Shivangi took another sip from the glass and said, "Yes, that was more than ten years back. I used to run an agency, Glamour Unlimited, in Kolkata. We used to groom models and actors, and also worked with casting agencies and production companies to create opportunities for our students. I realized that the opportunities in Kolkata were limited. The industry here was cash-strapped, and the producers had no interest in experimenting with new talent. I wanted to expand my business to Mumbai, which I thought was a better market."

"And Mr Chowdhury was supportive?"

"Oh yes, Ranjan never questions my judgement in these matters." Shivangi smiled.

"So, he came forward to finance the Mumbai operations of your agency."

"He did. I spent some time there to set up the office, hire staff, develop a few contacts – you know the drill. But, beyond a point, I realized that I could not continue to run the business the way I was doing. I was constantly travelling between Mumbai and Kolkata. I could not settle down in Mumbai as I could not leave Ranjan alone. We were running up hefty bills with flight tickets and hotel charges. Those were still early days, and we were not making enough money. So, I needed someone to take charge of the agency in Mumbai."

"Did you discuss your plans with Mr Chowdhury?"

"I did."

"Was that when he suggested that you hire Avigyan?"

"That's right. I was a bit surprised. Ranjan had mentioned him in the past. He was actually not happy that the boy had refused to stay with us while he studied in Kolkata. I barely knew him. But Ranjan said that the boy was family and he had not managed to find a job after passing out. Apparently, Avigyan was in dire straits, and he had called up Ranjan, asking for help. Honestly speaking, I was sceptical about the boy. He had studied commerce and did not know anything about the glamour industry. I thought that he was inexperienced and... and quite raw, you know what I mean?"

"Yes. I completely understand," said Agni.

"But you know, Mr Mitra, Ranjan was right. What Avigyan lacked in knowledge and experience, he made up for it in his passion and hard work, with some guidance and supervision. Till Mumbai got to his head!"

"What do you mean?"

"Well," Shivangi seemed to hesitate and then she said, "I don't know what went wrong. I heard rumours from some of the guys in the office that he had fallen in bad company. You see, Mr Mitra, it is easy to lose one's way when one starts earning money, when one is surrounded by glamour, and one has all the freedom in the world."

"I can imagine," said Agni. "When did you find out that things had started going south?"

"It was Ranjan who first realized that something was wrong. He had given Avigyan access to a joint bank account so that Avigyan could transact as and when he needed. Ranjan noticed large withdrawals and he checked with me. I was not aware where all that money was going. He wanted to look at the books, and the numbers did not add up. Ranjan smelt a rat and called Avigyan to his office in Kolkata."

"Were you there when they met in Mr Chowdhury's office in Kolkata?"

"No, I wasn't. Ranjan had said that he would deal with Avigyan alone. He had made it a point that they should meet in his office so that Avigyan realized that it was a business talk and not an uncle-nephew chit-chat."

"Do you know what happened?"

"I only know what Ranjan told me. Avigyan had not been able to explain the expenses and Ranjan had told him that he would stop financing the business."

"Where do you think the money was going?" asked Agni.

"We figured that Avigyan must have been spending the money on booze, women – the usual traps, you know. What difference would it make, knowing exactly how Avigyan was living it up with our hard-earned money?"

"Are you saying that you severed all ties with him thereafter? What happened to the agency?"

"Ranjan was gracious enough to let him run the business in Mumbai, although he made it very clear that he would not spend a single penny on that business any longer. Avigyan would have to manage on his own."

"What happened to your business in Kolkata?"

"It wasn't doing too well, in any case. After a couple of years, I pulled down the shutters."

"Was Avigyan in touch with you?"

"He did call me a few times after his showdown with Ranjan. He came up with ridiculous excuses and tried to convince me that Ranjan was being unreasonable. But, when I wanted him to explain to me what he had been doing with our money, he couldn't. Over the next few years, he called me now and then, asking for money. He could never muster the courage to call Ranjan for help. After some time, he stopped calling me as well."

"When was the last time he called you?"

"It's quite interesting, you know. After all these years, Avigyan called me about three weeks before his murder."

Agni remembered his conversation with Archana. He knew about the incident Shivangi was referring to. He asked, "Was it about money again?"

"It was. He said that he was planning to invest in a new business, and he needed money. He was going to partner with a friend and open a company that would produce web series for OTT platforms. He asked me if I could help him with the start-up investment. He explained to me that there were quite a few interesting projects in the pipeline and they were eyeing high returns."

"Did you help him?"

"I didn't," Shivangi smiled dryly. "I don't repeat mistakes, Mr Mitra. Running an NGO needs a lot of money. I would rather spend my money for a noble cause."

"Did you discuss this with Mr Chowdhury?"

"I did mention it to Ranjan. He supported me in my decision."

"Quite naturally," Agni nodded.

Shivangi looked at her watch, signalling that she had run out of time. "Mr Mitra, if you don't have any more questions, I am getting late for a meeting with the mayor."

Agni smiled to himself at the name-dropping. He did not let his amusement show and said, "No. I don't have anything else to ask, for now. You've been very helpful, Ms Chowdhury."

"You've been very kind too, Mr Mitra," Shivangi said as she stood up to leave, wiping the sweat off her face with a tissue. "May I ask you something?"

"Go ahead," Agni smiled.

"Would you be so kind to grace our annual event? I will send you a formal invitation."

"I would love to," Agni said, "unless something unforeseen comes up."

❖

Agni paced up and down the room with his arms behind him as Arya and he listened to the recording of Shivangi's statement. When it was over, Agni stopped and turned towards Arya.

"What do you think?" he asked.

"Obviously, she chose to hide facts."

"She did. I had'nt expected her to mention the blackmail threat over the slum fire incident anyway. However, she did not mention that she had actually gone to Ranjan Chowdhury's office three weeks before Avigyan's murder, asking for money on Avigyan's behalf. And that they had an argument! But there is something else that is bothering me."

"What is it?'

"You see, Arya, there is something fishy about the whole business of Avigyan running the agency in Mumbai and the misappropriation of funds. Till now, we've had three persons talk about it and everyone has a different take on the matter.

"Archana was the first one to tell us about Mr Chowdhury's ugly spat with Avigyan in his office eleven years back and his decision to stop funding the business in Mumbai. She told us that Shivangi had an argument in her husband's office about three weeks before Avigyan's murder over Avigyan's demand for more money and his threats of exposing Mr Chowdhury, which Archana had overheard. I had the feeling that Archana was hinting at some degree of leniency in Shivangi's behaviour towards Avigyan. Now, you may say that it was because of Archana's natural hatred for her lover's wife that she wanted to project Shivangi in a way that suited her narrative.

"Shivangi, on the other hand, clearly wanted to distance herself from the entire episode. According to her, it was Mr Chowdhury's decision to help his nephew while she had been sceptical from the beginning. It was Mr Chowdhury who had later found irregularities in the books and stopped funding the business after a heated altercation in his office with Avigyan, in her absence. She did not mention her argument with Mr Chowdhury at all.

"Finally, you will recall, when we spoke to Mr Chowdhury himself, he took a more neutral stand, not blaming anyone in particular. In fact, he never mentioned the showdown with Avigyan about financial irregularities and the fact that he had not been in touch with his nephew for years! From his statement, it seemed that everything had been fine between the two of them. He went to the extent of saying that, for him, Avigyan was the son he had never had!

"Why these discrepancies? I am waiting to hear from the computer forensics team. I hope Avigyan's laptop will finally throw some light on what exactly happened in Mumbai!"

25 Critical Evidence

Agni was busy going through case files and online archives of newspaper reports of the Netarhat shootout in 2010 that had killed Kingshuk Mukherjee and Siddhartha Bose, when the phone on his desk buzzed. It was Vishal from the computer forensics team.

Avigyan Chowdhury's laptop had been despatched by Inspector Sudhakar Joshi from Mumbai a few days back. Agni had immediately handed it over to the computer forensics team to break into the laptop and unearth everything that might be of relevance to the investigation. In modern times, electronic devices were an integral part of one's professional as well as personal lives, and over the last several years, Agni had observed that vital clues were to be unearthed in devices carefully secured by touch or retinal verification or by what the owners of such devices had believed were unbreakable passwords.

Nothing, however, was out of bounds for the expert team of computer forensics of his department. Vishal sounded excited on the phone. Agni was on his way to the computer forensics bay right away.

❖

When Agni reached Vishal's office, he found the somewhat nerdy young man, with a headful of black curls, overgrown stubble, and a green checked shirt thrown casually over a blue tee, hunched over a laptop, a bulky headphone around his ears, and his eyes darting frequently to a monitor in front of him. There was a pizza carton on the table, the last slice left and a half-empty glass of Coke with a pipe peeking out of an orifice in the plastic lid.

Vishal was so engrossed in his work that he had not noticed Agni walking into his cube and standing behind him. Agni gently patted his back, and he sat up straight with a start. He turned towards Agni and smiled, "Oh! I never noticed you, sir."

Agni smiled and pulled a chair next to Vishal. "You want to finish your lunch first?" he asked, pointing at the leftover slice of the pizza.

Vishal smiled sheepishly, and said, "It's alright. It's gone cold already."

"What have we got here?" asked Agni, looking at the laptop in front of Vishal.

Vishal cleared his throat and said, "A lot of stuff that has to do with Avigyan's business. Photographs of aspiring models and actors, applications, contracts, letters he had written to modelling agencies and production houses, invoices – all the regular stuff. I will walk you through all those some other time. Then, there are personal folders where we have the usual photos, movies and music files. However, there are two folders that I wanted you to look at immediately." He paused and drank through the pipe. Then, he continued, "Those two folders are protected by passwords."

With an air of suspense, Vishal wheeled his chair to the desk in front of him. With a few clicks of his mouse, he opened up a folder with a bunch of audio files. He passed on a headphone set to Agni.

The first audio clip Agni heard was a short message in a female voice. It went:

> *Mr Mukherjee, good morning. This is about your wife, Deboleena. If you think she has gone out just for a morning walk, you are being too naive. She's with her lover at Magnolia point right now. As a well-wisher, I thought that it was my duty to inform you.*

Agni turned towards Vishal and said. "Keep playing the clips – all of them."

There were three clips in all with a similar message. After playing all the clips back to back, Vishal stopped.

"Look at the timestamps of these files," said Vishal.

He pulled up the list of files in the folder. The three recordings were from alternate days in the month of January, in the year 2010. There were three more clips remaining.

Agni put the headphone back on. Vishal played the next clip.

The same woman, a different message, sounding more impatient this time, clearly meant to provoke the recipient to action:

> *Mr Mukherjee, good morning. Your wife is with her lover right now at Magnolia Point. But, you don't care, do you? You'd keep snoring in bed, and then let the slut play the ideal wife once she's back. Be a man, for god's sake! Go catch them while they are at it!*

The next message, with an air of urgency all through:

Hotel Repose?

I'd like to talk to Mr Siddhartha Bose, who's staying with you. It's very urgent!

<A few seconds' pause>

Mr Bose, I'm sorry to wake you up so early, but this is an emergency! I'm calling from Magnolia Point. There's a woman here, who I think is the forest officer's wife. She must have come here for a walk. She has fainted. I know you're a family friend. Please come here immediately. I tried calling Mr Mukherjee, but couldn't reach the phone at the bungalow.

The last message, with a tone of panic, went:

Sir, good morning. This is an emergency! There's a man holding a couple hostage near Magnolia Point. He has a gun.

Agni removed the headphone and kept looking at the screen, trying to tie those messages together, drumming the desk in front of him. After a couple of minutes, he turned towards Vishal. "Show me the timestamps of the last three clips," he said.

Vishal pulled up the list of files with their timestamps on the monitor. They were from 20 January 2010.

Agni thought for a while and then pulled out his phone.

He opened the list of his contacts and scrolled down to Debesh Roy.

Mr Roy took Agni's call after the second ring.

He sounded groggy. Agni looked at his watch and realized that Mr Roy had probably been having an afternoon nap.

"Mr Roy, good afternoon. This is Agni Mitra. I'm sorry if I woke you up," Agni tried to sound apologetic.

"It's alright," said Mr Roy. "It's almost time for my afternoon tea."

"I have a question for you. Do you remember the date when Kingshuk and his friend Siddhartha died in Netarhat?"

There was a brief silence at the other end of the line. Then, Mr Roy said, "How can I forget that day, Mr Mitra? It was the twentieth of January, 2010, a day after Debo's birthday."

"Thank you so much, Mr Roy," Agni ended the call.

Keeping his phone away, Agni turned towards Vishal and said, "You mentioned another folder that I should look at."

"Y...yes, sir," Vishal suddenly sounded somewhat uncomfortable. Agni wondered why.

He opened up a folder with several video clips. Almost instinctively, he pushed the laptop towards Agni by a few inches. As Agni put the headphone on, Vishal wheeled his chair back and stood up.

"You can watch the clips, sir. I'll be back in a minute," he stood up and headed towards the toilet.

Agni kept staring at his receding figure, somewhat perplexed. He then turned his chair around and diverted his attention to the laptop screen.

As Agni watched the first clip, his eyes widened and he understood why Vishal had decided to leave.

26 Mistaken Identities

Ranchi, Present Day

Agni walked out of the Birsa Munda Airport at Ranchi and stepped into the car that had been waiting for him. He had been told that Pratap Jha's house was close to the city centre, which was around seven kilometres from the airport. The traffic, however, was slow, and Agni had been warned that it could take longer than usual.

As the car made its way through congested roads, Agni noticed the bustling activity around him. Ranchi saw a sudden surge in population after the state of Jharkhand had been carved out.

❖

The doorbell rang, rousing Pratap Jha from his thoughts. It was not a common occurrence, an afternoon visitor. Pratap could not remember the last time he had friends coming over. Pratap did not have friends, for that matter.

"Who is it?" he called out, trying to raise his voice above the TV.

He muted the television and waited for an answer.

"This is ACP Agni Mitra. I am from Kolkata Police," came the reply from the door.

Pratap finished the glass of whiskey in a long swig and tried to remember, a deep furrow forming between his eyebrows. The name sounded familiar. After a few seconds, it came back to him. Of course, it was *that* detective from Kolkata. He had called a couple of days back.

He stood up with a groan and hollered, "Wait!" Walking on rubbery legs, he went to the cupboard and picked up a shirt. Then, he went to the front door and opened it.

Agni found it hard to believe that the man in front of him was the same dashing cop Pratap Jha, whose pictures he had seen in the reports in newspapers from ten years back. The man in front of him had unkempt grey hair that had thinned in places, a grey stubble several days old, bags under his eyes, a disproportionately large belly spilling over khaki shorts, and stale breath reeking of whiskey.

Pratap had hurriedly put on his shirt with buttons in the wrong holes, two open buttons at the bottom revealing his bulging paunch, and he was presently running his fingers through his hair, in an unsuccessful attempt to make himself look presentable. He did not look particularly happy to see Agni. Nevertheless, he stepped aside and let Agni walk in.

"Please come in, ACP... er..."

"Agni Mitra," Agni reminded him with a smile.

Agni followed him into a messy sitting room. Pratap cleared out a few newspapers from a chair, making space for Agni to sit.

There was a table in front of the other chair in the room. Agni saw a bottle of whiskey on the table and an empty glass.

Pratap sat down on the chair, facing Agni. He said, "To be honest, I'm just about to cook lunch, so..."

Agni read that as a polite way of saying 'Get lost!'. It was three in the afternoon and Agni found it quite surprising that the man was about to start cooking lunch.

Pratap asked, "So, what are you doing in Ranchi?"

Agni tried to sound apologetic and said, "Look, I'm genuinely sorry if this is a bad time. I can assure you that this won't take long. But I had to meet you in person and talk to you about a case I am currently investigating. I have reasons to believe that you have information that will help my investigation."

Pratap did not speak. He kept looking incredulously at Agni for almost a full minute, and then let out a chuckle, that made his belly jig. Agni was beginning to feel uncomfortable in the company of the man. He wondered if Pratap had his senses intact.

Agni looked around and asked hesitantly, "You live alone?"

Pratap smirked and said, "Wife left a few months after I had been thrown out. She thought I was no good, just a trigger-happy killer who would be a bad influence on our son."

Agni did not know how to respond.

"Can I get you something to drink?" Pratap asked.

"Thank you. That's very kind," Agni said. "A glass of water would be fine."

Agni saw Pratap's eyes wander to the bottle of whiskey. He smiled and said, "Or, something stronger if you prefer?"

Agni was mindful of the time of the day, and said, "No, thank you. A glass of water would suit me just fine."

Pratap went to the kitchen to get a glass. His mind drifted. What was the ACP doing in Ranchi? He wondered if he should be worried. But then, what was there to be worried about? He had nothing left to lose.

Pratap returned to the sitting room, filled the glass with water, and handed it over to Agni. He looked up to face Agni and asked, "So, ACP? What is it that you want to talk to me about?"

Agni finished the water in a long gulp and said, "Well, about the Netarhat firing in 2010 mainly."

Pratap suddenly looked miffed. He poured himself a tall drink and took a generous sip, grimacing as the drink burnt its way down his throat. He suppressed a belch and looked at Agni with pink eyes.

"What's there to talk about the firing, ACP … whatever? Is there anything that I haven't already repeated a thousand times? Or are there people who aren't happy with what they've already done to me?" He inched forward and brought his face close to Agni's and said, "Listen, I have nothing left to give. I've…. I've lost everything for that *one mistake*. I can only thank my stars that I was not hanged. But then, at times, I think, maybe that would have been better."

There was an awkward silence in the room, barring the creaking sound from the blades of the fan, and a crow outside.

Agni said, "Relax, Mr Jha. It isn't about you. It's about the woman." With a pause, he said, "She's dead."

Agni's words had the effect of pacifying Pratap, just a bit. He reclined in his chair, and put his hands behind his head, the posture having the effect of making his belly prominently stick out.

"Deboleena Mukherjee! That was her name. She's dead?" asked Pratap.

"Yes, she died from an overdose of sleeping pills," said Agni.

"Poor girl! She was so young when I – I..." Pratap hid his face in his palms for a few seconds. Agni allowed him time to cope with the news.

After a while, Pratap rubbed his eyes and the rest of his face with his palms and picked up the glass. He took another long sip and turned to Agni, "So, what do you want from me?"

"Pratap...can I call you that?" asked Agni before he continued.

"Yes, go ahead," came the reply.

"Pratap, I want to know from *you* what exactly happened in Netarhat ten years back. I have read the case reports, and the newspapers. But nothing matters to me more than the truth. I know that you are the only one who can give me that."

What Agni did not mention was that he knew that given Pratap's current state of mind, a phone call from Kolkata would not have served his purpose. Agni had to make him feel safe, and then coax and cajole him to pull the facts out.

Pratap took some time to speak. He did not want to trace his way back to those dark lanes in his mind, but he wanted to help the man in front of him get justice for the woman, whose life had been destroyed by an error in judgement at his end.

"You know what the state was going through at that time," Pratap spoke slowly. "The administration, the police, the security forces – the Maoists did not spare anyone. Even the local people lived in fear. Anyone the Maoists suspected of passing on information to the police or helping the forces would be brutally murdered, to serve as a warning for the others. We woke up every day to reports of landmine blasts, murders, kidnappings. But the police could not shy away from duty. We had to put on the uniform and walk into the battlefield every day, obeying orders that came from the top.

"That fateful morning, I received an anonymous call. The words still ring in my ears. I was told that, a man brandishing a gun had been seen holding a couple hostage near Magnolia Point."

"Was it *you* who received the call?"

"Yes, I did. You see, ACP, I had two choices. I could waste precious time trying to trace the caller, or get into action with my team. I considered the worst-case scenario and chose the latter. There were two lives at stake. Apparently, that was a mistake!" Pratap said sarcastically.

Agni nodded. He asked, "What happened next?"

"When we reached the spot, I did see a man with a gun, and a couple who seemed to be held hostage. Now, that's always a tricky situation. If the intention of the man was to kill the couple, then alerting him might have immediately led him to shoot. Instead, we started approaching him from behind. The plan was to take him by surprise and disarm him. I asked my men to hold fire, as we advanced.

"But the man fired, and the poor fellow with the woman took the bullet on his chest. *Then,* I fired at the man behind his knees, which brought him down. But, two other shots had already been fired and those hit him on his back as he fell. Those were the shots that took his life, not the one that I fired. But, as the man leading the mission, I had to take responsibility."

Pratap stopped speaking and sipped from his glass of whiskey. After a few seconds, he said, "And then, my nightmare started."

"I have a question," Agni interrupted. "Was it a man or a woman who made the call to the station that morning?"

"It was a woman."

"And did you manage to trace the call later?"

"No, we could not. It turned out that the call had been made over the internet. From a malicious website that let you make VoIP calls anonymously."

"I see," Agni said after a brief pause. "So, this was a case of mistaken identities."

"It was," Pratap sighed. "It turned out during the investigation that the man wielding the gun was Kingshuk Mukherjee, a forest officer. The woman was his wife, Deboleena Mukherjee. She used to teach music in a local school. The other man who was shot down by Kingshuk was a common friend, Siddhartha Bose. He was visiting them. Theirs was a fascinating story, which I got to know in course of the trial."

27 The Mysterious Caller

Netarhat, 2010

The trees around the bungalow stood like giant spears against the night sky, and the wind made a soft rushing sound as it passed through their leaves. The night was moonless, yet distinctly luminous with the stars in the clear sky. There was impenetrable silence all around, except the monotonous orchestra of crickets. There was no sign of life around the house, barring occasional noises of rodents scurrying in the bushes.

Siddhartha and Kingshuk were in the balcony, finishing their drinks. Deboleena was busy laying out plates on the dinner table.

Siddhartha worked for a coal dealer and visited Ranchi frequently. Almost on every occasion, he spent a few nights in Netarhat, and made sure that he visited Deboleena and Kingshuk in their forest department bungalow. He politely declined, every time Kingshuk asked him to stay with them.

Siddhartha insisted on staying at Hotel Repose, which was about a mile from the bungalow, very close to Magnolia Point.

Deboleena often wondered if Siddhartha still had feelings for her and therefore, felt awkward staying with them. So she respected his decision.

Today, of course, was special. It was 19 January, Deboleena's birthday. Ever since Siddhartha had taken up the job with the coal dealer, he had made it a point to be with the couple in Netarhat on Deboleena's birthday.

The evening had been spent in blissful bonhomie with delicious finger food and expensive spirits, accompanied by laughter and nostalgia. Deboleena and Siddhartha sang their favourite duets that flowed mellifluously through the forests surrounding the bungalow. Kingshuk, however, had barely spoken all evening. He had been engrossed in his drinks, nodding his head occasionally in appreciation as his wife and her friend sang without a care in the world. But then, he had always been quiet and reserved.

Siddhartha emptied his glass and looked at the wall clock. It was almost nine. The night was getting colder and there was a hilly terrain he would have to cross. The fog sometimes got too thick in these parts. Kingshuk, of course, had instructed his chauffeur to drop Siddhartha at his hotel.

"Hey birthday girl, I think it's time we started dinner," Siddhartha hollered to Deboleena.

"Dinner is ready, guys! If you're done with the whiskey," said Deboleena, smiling at Siddhartha from the dining area.

Kingshuk finished his drink and put his glass down on the table. The two men headed for the elaborate dinner that had been laid out.

"Kingshuk," Siddhartha cleared his throat and asked, as the three sat down for dinner. "You looked somewhat distracted all through the evening. Is everything alright?"

"I've been watching you for a couple of days, Kingshuk. Something is definitely wrong. You are not your usual self," added Deboleena. It seemed from her manner of speech that she had been too eager to ask, but had been waiting for someone to broach the topic.

Kingshuk smiled wryly, and said, "Well, I can tell you, if you insist..."

He stopped midway and turned towards Siddhartha. He asked, "Siddhartha, how long have you been here this time?"

"You forgot, already? It's been seven days, my friend."

"Seven days," Kingshuk repeated. He paused briefly and said, "Ever since you've come here, I've been receiving a rather strange phone call every other morning, around six thirty."

"Six thirty, every other day, for a week?" Deboleena put her fork down looking peeved. "And you never told me!"

"Yes," Kingshuk turned towards Deboleena. "You leave for your walk around six every morning. The call comes every other day about half an hour after you've left."

"Who's the caller?" asked Deboleena.

"I don't know. I've asked every time. But the caller simply disconnects the call after delivering the message."

"What's the message?" asked Siddhartha.

"The caller wants me to be watchful about a certain matter," Kingshuk said and looked alternately at Siddhartha and Deboleena. They had stopped eating and looked anxious. Kingshuk thought for a few seconds and seemed to change his mind. He tried unsuccessfully to force a laugh and said, "Come on! It must be someone playing a prank. Let's drop the topic. I won't let a trickster spoil Debo's birthday dinner."

Siddhartha asked, "Kingshuk, is it a man or a woman?"

"It's a woman," said Kingshuk. "She calls herself my 'well-wisher'."

"Now I know why you don't want to tell us more about the calls," Siddhartha winked. "So, there's a woman calling our friend every other morning after the wife goes out for a walk. Deboleena, I think *you* are the one who needs to be watchful here, and not the other way round!"

All three of them broke into laughter.

❖

A little while after dinner, Kingshuk's car pulled up in front of the bungalow. The temperature had dropped considerably, and a shroud of dense fog seemed to have surrounded the house. Siddhartha zipped up his woollen jacket and bade farewell to the couple.

"Deboleena, see if you can get your husband to confess about those calls," Siddhartha said as he got into the car. Deboleena laughed heartily while Kingshuk forced a dry smile.

Deboleena and Kingshuk walked up to the bedroom upstairs. As she made the bed, Deboleena asked Kingshuk, "Are you sure you don't want to tell me more about those calls?"

Kingshuk was in the small balcony adjacent to the room, smoking. He kept looking at the darkness and said, "No, not right now. Don't let this bother you. Let's wait a few more days. If it continues, then I'll do something about it."

Deboleena said, "Going by the pattern, she should call you tomorrow. Do you want me to stay back and take the call?"

Kingshuk finished the cigarette and stamped out the stub. He looked up at Deboleena and said, "That won't be necessary."

That very moment, the caller's words were ringing in Kingshuk's ears:

Mr Mukherjee, good morning. This is about your wife, Deboleena. If you think she has gone out just for a morning walk, you are being too naive. She's with her lover at Magnolia Point right now. As a well-wisher, I thought it was my duty to inform you.

❖

Siddhartha stopped and gasped for breath. His eyes kept looking for Deboleena. He had been running all the way from his hotel. The phone in Siddhartha's room had awakened him from deep sleep around 6:15 a.m.

Siddhartha was not a morning man. He went to bed late and woke up when the world had already busied itself. And now that he was on vacation, he had a legitimate reason to remain tucked in for as long as he felt like.

That morning, he had picked up the phone cursing the receptionist, and had mumbled an indignant "Hello". What he had heard from the woman at the other end of the line had made him sit up in a flash.

Mr Bose, I'm sorry to wake you up so early, but this is an emergency! I'm calling from Magnolia Point. There's a woman here, who I think is the forest officer's wife. She must have come here for a walk. She has fainted. I know you're a family friend. Please come here immediately. I tried calling Mr Mukherjee, but couldn't reach the phone at the bungalow.

Siddhartha had put on his clothes and left the hotel in the next five minutes. He would regret afterwards that he did not bother to call up Kingshuk's bungalow and verify what the caller had said.

Siddhartha called Deboleena by her name a few times. There was no trace of tourists at Magnolia Point at that hour of the morning. When he had reached a clearing, Siddhartha could finally see Deboleena. She was in her jogging attire, her hair tied back in a ponytail, her face flushed and glowing with the sweat.

Siddhartha ran towards her and asked frantically, “Are you alright?”

“Siddhartha, what are *you* doing here? Is everything okay? Of course, I am alright,” Deboleena looked startled.

“Deboleena, I got a call around 6:15 a.m. that you had come here for your walk and had fallen sick. The caller said that she had not been able to reach the phone at the bungalow.”

“I’m perfectly fine, Siddhartha,” Deboleena said, her voice shaking, as she could feel an unknown fear slowly taking her in its grip.

“Is that call you received somehow related to the calls Kingshuk has been receiving?” Those calls had been bothering her since last night.

Siddhartha thought for a few seconds and said, “More importantly, who’s the caller and where the hell did she call from? I don’t see a public phone booth or a shop anywhere near this place, from where she might have called. It seems that the caller knows us. She knows that you are here now. She knows that we are friends. She knows that I’m in Netarhat right now. She even knows which hotel I am staying in!

“I’ll need to check with the receptionist what exactly the caller had said when she had called the hotel, because there’s no direct line to the room.” Siddhartha banged his palm with his fist and said, “Actually, it was rather stupid of me to leave the hotel and come running all the way up here, without checking first with the receptionist or with Kingshuk. How could I let myself be fooled by that woman?”

Deboleena was still shaking. Siddhartha held her by her arms and said, "Actually, I was very worried for you. I... I wasn't thinking straight..." Deboleena looked into his eyes.

❖

The call came at the same time – about half an hour after Deboleena had gone out for her walk at six. There was a sense of urgency in the voice of the woman today:

> *Mr Mukherjee, good morning. Your wife is with her lover right now at Magnolia Point. But, you don't care, do you? You'd keep snoring in bed, and let the slut play the ideal wife once she's back. Be a man, for god's sake! Go catch them while they are at it!*

Like on all previous occasions, the call was disconnected before Kingshuk could ask the caller to divulge her identity.

Kingshuk kept looking at the crumpled sheet on Deboleena's side of the bed, lost in thought. The more he thought, the more he began to believe the caller. There was no doubt that there was a marked change in Deboleena's behaviour whenever Siddhartha was in town. His mind was filled with questions.

Was it just because the visit of an old friend was like a breath of fresh air in her otherwise monotonous life far away from the hustle and bustle of a big city where she had grown up? Or was there more to that exuberance with which she sang with Siddhartha every time they met? What made Siddhartha drop everything and turn up at their house every year for Deboleena's birthday? Or for that matter, every time he visited Ranchi on business? Why had the two of them looked so worried when he had mentioned last night that the caller wanted him to be watchful about a certain matter? Why had Deboleena even insisted on dealing with the caller herself?

Kingshuk also realized that it might not be prudent to dismiss the calls as someone's idea of playing a stupid prank simply because the caller seemed to know a lot about them. She did know their names, the phone number of his bungalow; she did know that Deboleena went for her walk around six every morning. She did know that Deboleena usually went in the direction of Magnolia Point for her walk. She did know that Siddhartha was in town. And she claimed that she knew about Deboleena and Siddhartha having an affair. How wise would it be to ignore just that once piece of information when everything else she knew about them was right?

Kingshuk made up his mind. It would indeed be too naïve of him to completely ignore the caller without checking at least once.

He would have to find out for himself, although the very thought of finding Deboleena in the company of Siddhartha at Magnolia Point at this hour of the day, if the caller was right, made his skin crawl. But then, what if the caller *was* right?

❖

Kingshuk clenched his fist and walked towards the steel chest. He opened it and picked up the gun which the department had given him for his own protection in the event of a threat. He had never had a reason so far to use it, the current situation in the state notwithstanding. Maybe, he would find a reason today, because in his mind, Kingshuk was sure about what he would do if the caller was proved to be right. Adultery, for him, was unpardonable!

He put on a sweater and jumped into his jeep in a flash, without bothering to wake the driver up. The sky was clearing, and there was a chill in the air. But the icy wind seemed to fan the fire burning in Kingshuk's heart as he drove towards Magnolia Point like a maniac.

Kingshuk parked his jeep away from the clearing behind a sal tree, and stepped out. His hand reached back to feel the pistol pushed down the small of his back under his pants. As he now inched towards the clearing, he could clearly see Siddhartha and Deboleena. Siddhartha was holding Deboleena by her arms. He could hear Deboleena speaking, "Siddhartha, I think we must talk to Kingshuk. There's no point wasting time ..."

Kingshuk walked into the clearing and raised his gun at his wife and her lover.

"You are right, Debo. There's indeed no point wasting time," he thundered. "I was such an idiot to trust my wife and her friend, even after I had been warned."

"Kingshuk, what are you talking about? Are you out of your mind?" screamed Deboleena, as she freed herself and walked towards Kingshuk, who had his gun trained firmly on Siddhartha.

"Enough, Debo! I've had enough of your play-acting," said Kingshuk, his eyes blood-shot, his unruly hair ruffled by the morning breeze, the muscles in his arm taut, as he released the lock of his gun.

"Just for my curiosity, how long has this been going on? Siddhartha, I knew you had feelings for Deboleena when we were in college. But when I welcomed you into my home, I made the mistake of assuming that you had managed to put all that behind you and moved on. Apparently, you hadn't. And Deboleena, looks like you suddenly discovered your love for this man here, feelings which had been lying dormant for years. The feelings were so strong that you decided to throw caution to the wind and cheat on your husband!" Kingshuk stopped only to breathe, shaking in rage, sweating even in the morning chill.

"Please, Kingshuk! Listen to me! You're making a big mistake. There's a conspiracy. Someone's trying to mess up our lives!" Deboleena pleaded with her hands folded. Siddhartha wanted to explain, but his words failed him. The wind howled through the tall trees around them.

"Kingshuk, you've got it all wrong! I... I can explain..." Siddhartha finally managed to speak, Kingshuk's pistol still pointed at him.

"You fucking son-of-a-bitch! How could you even imagine that you would get away by fooling me?" Kingshuk cried out as he pressed the trigger.

None of the three had heard the heavy police boots approaching the clearing from the direction of the forest.

28 The Mastermind

Kolkata, Present Day

Debesh Roy led Agni and Arya into his study. He sat behind a desk that was untidy with files and papers carelessly thrown all over. There was a reading lamp that managed to light up just the pages of the book on the table, which he had been reading. The rest of the room was almost completely dark.

The sky outside the only window in the room had turned orange, as daylight slowly faded away. The trees surrounding the apartment block were tossing their heads in the breeze. The traffic could be heard on the busy road below as the city went about its business.

Mr Roy looked pale and weak, his grey hair dishevelled. He gestured to Agni and Arya to sit on two chairs across the desk. Agni's eyes went to a framed picture in black-and-white, sitting on the desk – of a young boy and a younger girl.

Mr Roy followed Agni's eyes and said, "That's Debo and me when I was in high school. We were on a vacation in Nainital." A more recent picture of Deboleena Mukherjee was on the dimly lit wall behind, a fresh garland around it.

"Are you feeling better now, Mr Roy?" asked Agni.

Mr Roy took a while to reply. He said, "The body heals, Mr Mitra. But what can you do with the heart?"

Agni nodded. He knew what Mr Roy meant. He had been looking for the answer himself.

"Mr Roy, we tend to credit time with healing powers. I am yet to experience it first-hand, though." Agni smiled. He sat up straight and then asked in a voice which had turned business-like very quickly, "I won't spend a lot of time beating about the bush here. I need to ask you a few questions, as I told you when I called."

"Go ahead," Mr Roy said nonchalantly.

"Is it true that your business is not doing too well? That you are neck deep in debt. That your family doesn't stay with you. And these are possibly the reasons why you suffer from chronic depression?"

Mr Roy who had momentarily cast his eyes on the pages of the book in front of him, looked up. His eyes looked tired in the light of the reading lamp. His facial muscles looked taut, as if he had suddenly been alerted of a possible attack and was readying himself to fight. "Who told you?" he asked.

"That's not important," replied Agni.

With a deep sigh, Mr Roy ran his fingers through his hair and said, "Mr Mitra, I'm sorry, but I have to say that these are extremely personal questions. What have these questions got to do with your investigation?"

Agni did not answer the question and said, "Mr Roy, isn't it true that Ms Mukherjee's property, which she had inherited from her husband and your father, will pass on to you, by default, now that she is no more? This couldn't have happened at a better time for your business!"

Agni saw the colour rise to Mr Roy's cheeks. He narrowed his eyes and thumped the desk so hard that a few sheets of paper flew over and landed on the floor.

"What are you hinting at, Mr Mitra? This is absolutely disgusting! Is this what your investigation has led to? Is this the best that the celebrity detective can manage?"

Instead of answering the question, Agni said, "Mr Roy, let's get this straight. I'm the one who asks the questions here. You cannot deny the facts that you stand to gain monetarily from the death of your sister, and that you chose to hide information from me. I want you to tell me why exactly you visited Ms Mukherjee's residence on the morning of her death."

"You asked me the other day, and I answered," Mr Roy snarled.

"I apologise for repeating the question, but I have to ask you again, as you were not entirely honest with your answer the other day, Mr Roy," said Agni.

"What do you mean?" Mr Roy asked, running his tongue over his parched lips.

"You told me that your visit to Ms Mukherjee's house on the morning of her death was routine. You do travel now and then to the other end of the city to check on her. You consider that your responsibility as a caring elder brother," Agni paused.

"Yes... yes, that's right," said Mr Roy.

"But, that morning, you did not drive all the way to New Town from Tollygunge just to check on your sister.

Ms Mukherjee's behaviour that morning was also not normal. The two of you actually had an argument that morning. You warned your sister that she did not know what she was getting into. This has been confirmed by Manoj and Pratima. Then, you called your sister *twenty-seven times* in course of the day, which again, is not normal, going by the records of Ms Mukherjee's calls from the last three months."

"What are you trying to prove?" Mr Roy tried to sound defiant, but his voice had lost its strength.

There was a glass bottle half filled with water on the table, and an empty glass turned upside down. Agni picked up the glass, filled it with water, and pushed it towards Mr Roy. He picked up the glass with trembling fingers and emptied it in a long gulp. He wiped his mouth with the back of his hand.

Agni continued, "When I met advocate Tarun Bakshi who was not just Ms Mukherjee's lawyer, but had also been a close friend of your father, he told me about the difficulties you have been facing in your business for some time. I also came to know that since Ms Mukherjee had not remarried, did not have children and had not made a will, her property would pass on, by default, to you. That does sound pretty convincing as motive for murder, what do you think, Mr Roy?"

Mr Roy did not answer. He shifted uncomfortably in his chair. The only sound in the room was of Mr Roy's wheezing. Agni went on, "The forensics team found traces of the powdered drug on the bar top. Someone had powdered the tablets and added them to the wine glasses that night."

Mr Roy looked into Agni's eyes and said, "I did not kill my sister, Mr Mitra. You haven't managed to solve this case and you are probably running out of time. You are trying to set me up for a crime I can't even dream of."

Agni smiled and said, "Relax, Mr Roy. I am not done yet. We learnt from the forensics experts that the drug had been found in the wine glasses that the two had been drinking from, *but not in the bottle*. Also, one of the glasses had fingerprints of both Avigyan and Ms Mukherjee, and the other had the fingerprints of only Ms Mukherjee, which suggest that, no one else had handled the glasses that night.

"All these findings prove beyond doubt two things. One, the sedatives were added when the wine was poured into the glasses that night by Ms Mukherjee, but not into the bottle earlier, with a possible intention to kill anyone who drinks from that bottle.

"Second, it was Ms Mukherjee herself who had made the drinks that night."

There was pin-drop silence in the room, but for the sounds of the laboured breathing of Mr Roy. Agni continued, "This can mean only one thing. Ms Mukherjee was not murdered. Instead, it was she who invited Avigyan Chowdhury to her house for the night and put the overdose of sleeping pills in his drink. She had planned to end her own life as well as she had not wanted to live through another murder trial, this time as the suspect. The reason for her planning to murder Avigyan Chowdhury became perfectly clear when I examined Avigyan's laptop and later visited Ranchi to meet ex-inspector Pratap Jha."

Agni stood up and bent over the table, his face level with Mr Roy's. He said almost in whispers, "You did not kill anybody, but you did know that your sister had planned to kill Avigyan Chowdhury, didn't you? Why else would you warn her that morning? Why else did you call her twenty-seven times through the day, trying to dissuade her? Do not deny. Do not make it more difficult for yourself.

"In fact, your heart failure the next morning was not as much from the shock of learning about your sister's death as it was from regret. You had known about Ms Mukherjee's plan all along and yet, you had not been able to talk her out of it."

Mr Roy's face was contorted, and his eyes welled up. He buried his face in his palms and said almost in whispers after a while, "Debo came to know that it was Avigyan who had been the mastermind behind the killings of Kingshuk and Siddhartha in Netarhat. She came up with the plan and discussed with me. I tried to talk her out of it, but she would not listen. I had to give up finally."

"None of this justifies your decision to *not* inform the police," said Agni.

"To be fair to Debo, that farcical trial had been a waste of everyone's time, Mr Mitra! The cop lost his job, but they never figured out who had made those calls that morning. Someone had to deliver justice. Debo took it upon herself," Mr Roy looked up with blood-shot eyes and a smirk on his face, "I knew that she was breaking the law, but I had no respect left for it anymore."

Agni smiled dryly and said, "That still makes you an accomplice to the crime and the law of the land will take its own course, Mr Roy. Here's your arrest warrant." Agni put the warrant on the table and said, "You'll have to come with us."

Mr Roy's wheezing had intensified, and his shoulders drooped ominously. He was struggling to breathe and began to sweat profusely. Sweat patches began to appear on the kurta he was wearing. He clutched his chest in pain.

"Call an ambulance, Arya!" Agni screamed and rushed to Mr Roy's side, putting an arm around his shoulders.

❖

After the ambulance had left with Mr Roy, Arya said, "Agni, I get it that it was Avigyan who had planned the massacre at Netarhat ten years back and Ms Mukherjee avenged the murders of Kingshuk and Siddhartha by poisoning him.

"How did you get to know? *But more importantly, how did Ms Mukherjee get to know?*" He paused and thought for a few seconds, then added, "And what about the shooting? Who planned it and why? Where does Wajid Shamim come in?"

Agni smiled and patted Arya on his shoulder. He said, "All in good time, my friend!"

29 | Sinister Plan

Mumbai, 2010

My trip to Kolkata a few months back was disastrous. The "anomalies" in the books had not escaped my uncle's attention, and he was livid. He said that I was incompetent and useless. Had it not been for him, I would have been on the roads. He went on to say that I was ungrateful, and like my father, a disgrace to the family. However, none of his relentless rants really mattered.

The old fool was letting some steam off. That was what I kept telling myself. However, I felt the earth slipping under my feet with what he said next. He would not finance the business anymore! He had already discussed his plan with his wife, and apparently, she was absolutely fine. What a bitch!

That was the moment when I lost my cool. I said that he had no right to do that to me. That agency was my livelihood. He could not just wake up one fine morning and decide to pull the plug. He should have notified me well in advance, so that I could find another job.

There were still a couple of clients I had been talking to, and I could not just pull the shutters down. I realized after exactly twenty minutes – one could not miss that wall clock in his chamber with the picture of the Swiss Alps on its dial and my eyes were drawn to that clock time and again as we argued – that I had been screaming at the top of my voice. His secretary had knocked on the door of his chamber and had peeped in a couple of times, probably to make sure that I was not strangling the boss.

Now, here is the thing with bullies. You shout back at them and they cower like chickens. The same happened with that stupid old jerk. He calmed down, helped himself to a glass of water, wiped his brow and struck a deal with me.

He said that he would let me run the agency. I could retain the office and the staff and continue to work with the handful of clients I had managed to bring in since the time I had taken over. He would clear all the dues once and for all as his wife's name was also getting smeared. But going ahead, he or his wife would have nothing to do with the business. I would have to run it on my own. I could steer the business in whichever direction I wanted to.

I took it up as a challenge and left his office.

On my way out, I took a close look at the secretary. I wondered if she was fucking my uncle, and then I wondered if he still managed to get it up.

❖

As I sipped on cheap whiskey and gorged on tepid chicken pakoras in that dingy bar with its blue and green lighting, uncomfortable wooden chairs, dirty floral-print tablecloths with stains all over, raunchy Bollywood numbers blaring from hidden speakers, I remembered the day I lost the backing of my rich uncle. Siddhartha sat right opposite and kept talking about the coal dealer he worked for. He had come to Mumbai on business and had wanted to meet his 'campus buddy' over drinks. Jasmine Bar-cum-Restaurant, of course, was my suggestion. I did not want him to pay for the drinks, and I could not afford a more expensive place.

We finished the drinks and stepped out.

It was quite late. I looked at the thinning crowd on the beach and at the gaudily decked-up stalls selling golas and pav-bhaji. The arc of the Marine Drive – the Queen's Necklace – and the specks of Mumbai lights in the distant horizon were before us. The refreshing wind swept through our hair, as cars swooshed down the road. We walked along the promenade, lined with palm trees.

"Tell me about your love life," Siddhartha said sarcastically. "You must be living it up here!"

I was almost going to tell him about Shona, and then I held myself back. Instead I asked, "Are you in touch with Deboleena?"

"Guess what? I am!" Siddhartha said triumphantly. I looked at him, unbelievingly.

"Actually, Kingshuk and Deboleena are now in Netarhat. Kingshuk is posted there as a forest officer. Deboleena teaches music in a school. They live in a beautiful forest department bungalow," Siddhartha went on. This was sounding like a fucking fairy tale!

"Do you meet her?" I asked, nervously. I would not be able to bear it, if he said that he did.

"Oh yes, every time I am in Ranchi," he said. Those were the exact words I did not want to hear. My blood began to boil, and I was scared of myself. I had to be calm, I reminded myself, and clenched my jaws. The bastard went on, "You should see her! Hasn't aged a day since the time you saw her last. She is very disciplined. Runs every morning. Gets up sharp at six! Actually, their bungalow is pretty close to Magnolia Point, you know. Now, you know me, don't you? I can't even dream of getting up so early! I manage to get off my bed around ten! With a lot of difficulty," Siddhartha guffawed.

I looked at the boulders by the beach and wondered if I would feel better, if I could smash his head on one of those.

"Do you stay with them when you are in Ranchi?" I asked.

"Kingshuk keeps asking me to. But, I don't. I put up at Hotel Repose which is close to their house. I usually have dinner with them every night when I'm there," Siddhartha said. I pushed my hands into the pockets of my trousers, so that they did not reach for his throat.

"It's her birthday on the nineteenth of this month. I'll be reaching a week in advance."

I could not speak. "Still love her, do you?" Siddhartha nudged me, his elbow digging into my ribs. I did not reply. "Come on, you can tell me," Siddhartha said. He was getting on my nerves but I remained silent.

"Okay, talk to her," Siddhartha suddenly stopped walking and pulled out his phone. He went to his list of contacts and started scrolling down. "I have the number of their bungalow."

He pulled up the number and thrust the phone into my hand. "Here," he said, "Call them. They would be in bed by now. It would be fun if Kingshuk picks up. I want to hear you telling him *that you're missing his wife!" Siddhartha laughed so much that he had tears in his eyes.*

"Come on, come on... make that call!" Siddhartha said with the same earnestness as a child pleading with its father for an ice-cream. He wanted this to be his entertainment for the night. "You are such a fucking coward!" he tried to provoke me when he realized that I would not make that call.

I stood there, rooted to the spot, my eyes fixed on the number on the phone as it got stamped on my brain. Tears stung my eyes, and I was not sure how long I would be able to hold them back.

I thrust the phone into Siddhartha's shirt pocket and walked towards the road. There was an autorickshaw approaching. I signalled to the driver.

"Come on, yaar! You took it to your heart. I was only joking!" I could hear Siddhartha calling after me. I felt a rush of fury. Why did life have to be so unfair? There I was, destroying myself in the memory of the woman who had, in all probability, completely forgotten me. And Siddhartha was the privileged one, getting to meet her, to have dinner with her family and to celebrate her birthdays!

I did not look back. I got into the autorickshaw and hid my face in my palms. The tears finally broke free and now, there was no stopping them.

❖

Later that night, I was restless in bed as sleep eluded me. The hum of the fan, the rustle of the bed sheet and the creaks of the bed as I tossed and turned were the only sounds in the room. The pill had relieved the headache but I could feel a storm brewing inside my heart. A string of facts kept circling in my mind – ones that I had gathered from Siddhartha's stupid banter. I was surprised at how much I had suddenly got to know about Deboleena.

Kingshuk and Deboleena were in Netarhat. Kingshuk worked as a forest officer and stayed in a forest Department bungalow whose phone number I now had. Theirs was a fairy-tale life. Deboleena was as beautiful as ever. She was disciplined and took care of herself. Her day started with a jog to Magnolia Point at six in the morning. Siddhartha visited them frequently. He stayed at Hotel Repose close to Magnolia Point. He was planning to be in Netarhat a week before Deboleena's birthday – 19 January. They were in Jharkhand, a state torn apart by the Maoist movement. Bomb blasts, murders, kidnappings. Anything could happen to anyone, anytime.

I remembered the way Siddhartha had ridiculed me a few hours back. I began to feel that destiny had made the three of them gang up against me, trampling my emotions mercilessly under their feet. But I was not going to be a mute spectator and languish in my pigeonhole in Mumbai anymore. Every single one of them would have to pay.

I sat up straight. The pieces had come together in a whole, slowly germinating into a sinister plan. I got off the bed and started pacing up and down the room as the plan took shape in my mind. There were still a few things that might be left to chance, but then, I had nothing to lose. All it needed were a few phone calls. I could use one of those Internet sites from where one could make anonymous calls.

But, wait! It would still be my voice. What if Siddhartha recognized my voice, my accent that they made fun of? No, there was no way I could make those calls. I needed someone else to make those calls for me. Someone I could trust. Or, someone who could be forced to be an accomplice to my grand plan through threats or through blackmail. The later sounded like a safer plan – you could never trust anyone when you were planning murders.

My eyes went to the laptop, loaded with videos of my romps with Shona, in that very room, on that very bed. Maybe those videos were destined to serve a different purpose beyond helping me jerk off before I went to sleep every night. I imagined the look of horror, disgust and shame on Shona's face, sitting next to me inside my room, when she saw the videos. She would be ready to do anything for me.

❖

I decided to call Shona the next morning. Then, I remembered that it was she who had insisted that I should call her by that name as it made her feel 'loved'. She wanted me to be the only one who called her by that name. Well, there obviously was no love lost between us now.

It was time I started calling my aunt by her real name – Shivangi Chowdhury.

30 The Penthouse

Kolkata, Present Day

Agni saw Arya making his way towards him through the crowd. He looked excited.

"We carried out the search, Agni. You were right. The room was bugged," he said the moment he had caught up with Agni. Agni winked and said, "Great job, Arya! Everything makes sense now."

"When did you reach?" asked Arya, realizing that Agni was not going to elaborate on the implications of Arya's findings earlier in the day.

"It has been about ten minutes," said Agni, looking at his watch.

The annual event of Hope Foundation had ended about half an hour back. Shivangi Chowdhury, resplendent in a green evening dress that clung to her meticulously maintained contours, was busy posing with the mayor, as press photographers clicked away.

Agni had also noticed a few political leaders from the ruling party and celebrities from the entertainment industry whose presence had elevated the status of the event. He had been trying hard to stay away from prying lenses and waiting patiently to talk to Shivangi. His phone buzzed. He signalled at Arya and moved away to a relatively quieter place. He pulled out his phone from the pocket of his blazer and looked at the screen. He was surprised to see Archana's name flashing.

"Hello," said Agni.

"Thank god you took the call," Archana said in whispers, her voice shaking. She talked very fast, and though her voice did not rise above the din around, Agni did not miss the panic in her voice.

Agni moved further away from the hubbub and said, "Archana, listen to me. Just calm down, ok? Where are you calling from?"

"I... I'm in Ranjan's penthouse in New Town. Can you come over as soon as you can? I am sending you the Google Maps link."

"What's the matter?" asked Agni. New Town was not too far from The Hyatt.

"Ranjan has come to know that Wajid Shamim is in your custody. He's very worried that the police would make Wajid confess to his crimes, and Ranjan's name would come up. He thinks it won't be long before he's arrested as well and he's planning to leave the country tonight," Archana whispered into the phone.

"But, I'm scared because he has also come to know that I met you without his permission. He has been suspicious ever since he saw us talking, the day you visited him in the office. I didn't know he had got someone to tail me since that day! He called me over to the penthouse sometime back. He's drunk, and he's behaving strangely. He... he has even beaten me. I'm very scared right now, Mr Mitra. I have a feeling he is going to harm me in some way before he flees the country."

"Where are you making this call from?" asked Agni, looking at the other end of the lobby. The mayor had departed, and the crowd around Shivangi was thinning.

"I'm calling you from the bathroom. I don't have time. I'll send you the link to the location," Archana ended the call hastily.

Agni went running to Arya.

"Arya, get the car. We'll have to leave right now. I'll get Ms Chowdhury," Agni was already running in her direction.

"Thank you so much for coming, Mr Mitra," Shivangi saw Agni and stepped forward, her face lit up by her smile. She said, "I'm so sorry you had to wait! Did you get to watch the programme? Those children..."

Agni did not let her finish and said, "Ms Chowdhury, we'll talk later, but for now, you'll have to come with me. We don't have time on our hands."

"Oh!" Shivangi looked surprised, "But I had a few things to take care of."

"I told you, we don't have time!" Agni said sternly, the sudden change in his demeanour taking Shivangi by surprise, "Please follow me!" Agni was already walking towards the exit of the hotel.

Shivangi gestured to an assistant and started following Agni in brisk steps. When she had almost bridged the gap, she asked, "Mr Mitra, where are we going?"

Agni did not look back and said, "To your husband's penthouse in New Town."

"Ranjan's penthouse? Why are we going there?" asked Shivangi.

Agni had already got into the car waiting outside.

❖

Agni turned sharply around a bend, the tyres screeching to a halt on the brown, dusty road. Getting off the car, Agni ran towards the apartment complex that stood in the middle of nowhere. Arya and Shivangi followed him. Agni flashed his ID at the security guard. He looked at his watch and ran towards the furthest tower. There were duplex penthouses in every tower. Ranjan Chowdhury had the topmost penthouse in the tower Agni ran into.

A family of six was trying to get into a small elevator. Agni flashed his ID and screamed, "Police! Get out of the way." The women and children stepped out of the elevator immediately. One of the two men blocked the door and said, "What nonsense is this? I will not tolerate police atrocities. Show me one reason why, as a taxpaying citizen of this country, I should..."

Agni pulled out his gun and snarled, "There are six reasons right inside this gun." The man moved aside without a word. Getting inside, Agni pressed the button for the twenty-ninth floor.

As soon as the 'ding' of the elevator announced that they had reached, Agni stepped out and ran towards the door in front of them. It was locked. Agni knocked gently. There was no response. Agni knocked again. This time, they could hear hurried footsteps inside.

When Archana opened the door, she presented a shocking sight the three had been least prepared for. Her hair was dishevelled, her eyes were swollen from crying, her kohl was smudged and formed dark trails down her flushed cheeks, a part of her upper lip was split where Ranjan Chowdhury's blows must have landed. She was struggling to hold her tears back, and all that could be heard were her muffled sobs.

"So, the two of you have turned the penthouse into your love nest!" Shivangi said with a smirk. "Your boss is into sadism these days, is he? You look miserable!" She stormed inside without waiting for Archana's reply, and began to peep inside the bedrooms.

Agni saw that they were in a hall – a sofa set, a low coffee table, a television on the wall facing the sofa, a door at the other end that led to a balcony, and beyond the balcony, an ink-blue evening sky. There were two trolley bags, ready for their journey overseas.

"Where is he?" Agni turned towards Archana and asked.

"He roughed me up and went up to the terrace with his bottle. He's out of his mind!" Archana said in whispers between her sobs. "He's going to come back anytime now. He'll kill me if he finds out that I called you. Please help me."

"Arya, stay here and look after her," Agni said and turned around. He ran towards the staircase that went up to the terrace.

31 | The Devious Conspiracy

"You? How the fuck did you...," Ranjan Chowdhury was shocked when he saw Agni on the terrace, sparsely lit by a few electric bulbs here and there. He was reclining on a deck chair, the electronic cigarette between his fingers, a bottle of whiskey on a low table next to him.

There were a couple of chairs around him. The wind moaned in Agni's ears as it blew over the empty stretches of land around the apartment complex.

Mr Chowdhury picked up the bottle, stood up with some effort and walked towards Agni with unsteady steps. He brought his face close to Agni's, the whiskey fumes in his foul breath nauseating, and said, "I can't believe the bitch had the guts to call you here! My mistake. I should have smashed her fucking phone, and then, her skull!"

"Well, Mr Chowdhury, tough luck you didn't, and now it's too late," Agni said with a smile. "My colleague is now with her and I have already asked for reinforcement. There's a change of plans, by the way. You're not going anywhere tonight. You're coming with me."

"Take it easy, Sherlock fucking Holmes," Mr Chowdhury dragged on his electronic cigarette and said disdainfully. "You have nothing against me!"

"In fact, I do. The question is, where do I start from?" said Agni. He was momentarily distracted by the sound of heels clicking behind him and turned around to see Shivangi on the rooftop. The smirk vanished from Mr Chowdhury's face the moment he saw his wife.

"You? What... what brings you here?" he stammered. He turned towards Agni and asked, "Why is she here?"

"I brought her here, Mr Chowdhury, because she needs to be around when you and I talk."

Agni sat down on one of the empty deck chairs, gesturing at Shivangi to grab the other. He said, "Mr Chowdhury, let me tell you a story. The story starts about ten years back with an unfortunate incident at Netarhat in the state of Jharkhand. The state at that time was bleeding from the Maoist movement. Bomb blasts, shootouts, kidnappings were common.

"On a cold morning in January, the police received information that a couple had been taken hostage by a terrorist near Magnolia Point, which happens to be a tourist attraction, famous for beautiful views of the sunset. The officer in charge, Pratap Jha, did not have the time to verify the authenticity of the call and rushed to the spot with his force. He, indeed, saw a man wielding a gun at a couple. From a distance, the couple seemed to be pleading for release. When the suspected terrorist fired at the man, the former was shot at and killed by the police, though that was not what Pratap had intended, his notoriety as an encounter specialist notwithstanding.

"It was later found out that the police had made a mistake. The man wielding the gun was not a terrorist, but a forest officer by the name of Kingshuk Mukherjee. The couple whom the police had assumed had been taken hostage were Deboleena Mukherjee, the wife of the forest officer and a music teacher in the local school, and her friend, Siddhartha Bose, who worked for a coal dealer and was in Ranchi on business, visiting Deboleena on her birthday.

"The police never managed to find out the identity of the caller, as the calls had been made from one of those websites that allow you to make anonymous calls over VoIP. Pratap Jha lost his job and was abandoned by his family. Today, he lives the life of a recluse. I met him a couple of days back in Ranchi."

Mr Chowdhury began to get up from his chair and said, "Look, Mr Mitra, I do not have the time for your *Crime Patrol*-type story. I have a lot of things to do."

"Such as killing your secretary and fleeing the country, I assume," Agni pulled out his gun and aimed it at Mr Chowdhury, "I told you. You are not going anywhere tonight! Let me finish my story *without interruptions*." Agni cleared his throat and said, "You see, the shootout was planned and executed as a conspiracy to eliminate Kingshuk Mukherjee and Siddhartha Bose. It was the brainchild of your nephew Avigyan Chowdhury."

"Hold on, Mr Mitra! Are you trying to suggest that I had a role to play in that shootout, just because it was my nephew who was the mastermind?" Mr Chowdhury asked angrily.

"No, Mr Chowdhury. I am not suggesting that you were involved in the conspiracy ten years back. I want to know, when exactly did you come to know about it?"

32 The Hitman's Contract

The colour vanished from Mr Chowdhury's face. He reached for the bottle of whiskey, but he had already emptied it. He licked his dry lips and tried to put up a brave front. He said, "Well... even if I did, is that a crime?"

"Relax, Mr Chowdhury. We will get there. But, didn't you come to know some time back that Avigyan was the mastermind behind the killings of Kingshuk Mukherjee and Siddhartha Bose?"

There was a moment's silence and then Mr Chowdhury said, "I... I did."

"When was that?"

"About two weeks before Avigyan's death," Mr Chowdhury said.

"That brings me to the important question. What did you do with that information?" Agni smiled.

Mr Chowdhury looked insolently at Agni, but did not respond.

"Let me refresh your memory," Agni said. "Avigyan had threatened you about a week before you came to know about the conspiracy and his role in it that he would expose your involvement in a slum fire incident, unless you paid him the money he needed to invest in a new business. That, of course, was a reference to the barbaric crime, for which you had hired Wajid Shamim, who had killed a social worker by the name of Ankita Guha, and had set a slum on fire, killing women, children and the aged who could not run for their lives that night. Avigyan, of course, had not threatened you directly. The message had been conveyed to you in your office by Ms Chowdhury, along with Avigyan's demand for money."

Mr Chowdhury's face was ashen. He muttered, "How do you know? Archana must have told you. The bitch will have to pay dearly for this!"

Agni did not bother to react and said, "You pulled the right strings and got away a few years back. But, if the case is reopened, you may not be as lucky this time. So, Avigyan had to be silenced because you were in no mood to pay him any money," Agni paused briefly for effect and said, "But, you were cautious. You must have wondered if there was wisdom in hiring Wajid to eliminate Avigyan. Wajid was known to be your hitman. Also, it was an open secret among people close to you that you had not been on good terms with Avigyan for years. Most importantly, your wife already knew that Avigyan had threatened you and it wouldn't take her a lot to put two and two together. Therefore, when you came to know about the incident at Netarhat, you decided to use that information to your advantage."

The wind roared across the roof, and the empty whiskey bottle toppled over to the floor and rolled along noisily.

"You got in touch with Ms Deboleena Mukherjee. You told her how the murders at Netarhat had been planned by Avigyan. You provoked her to avenge the murders of her husband and a dear friend. I would not be surprised if you had assured her of all the help that she would need to exact her vengeance. Ms Mukherjee did not count on your help, though. Instead, she made her own plan. She put an overdose of sedatives in the wine that she served that night to Avigyan after she had invited him to her house."

"I... I had nothing to do with Deboleena." Mr Chowdhury tried to put up a weak protest.

"As I formulated my theory, an examination of Ms Mukherjee's call records revealed that there had been numerous interactions between the two of you, starting around two weeks before Avigyan's murder. The calls started after you had come to know about the shootout in Netarhat."

Mr Chowdhury slumped deeper in the deck chair. It seemed he had lost the strength to put up a fight.

"Mr Chowdhury, it's in your best interest to cooperate with me. As you must be aware, Wajid Shamim is in our custody and he is ready to sing so that his own sentence is eased. All the heinous crimes that you had been hiring him for, over the years, including the slum fire incident are just waiting to be exposed."

Mr Chowdhury did not speak for a few minutes. Then, he looked up at Agni with tired eyes and said, "Mr Mitra, I agree that I met Deboleena and passed on the information that it was Avigyan who had planned the killings at Netarhat."

"But your real motive was far from humanitarian, Mr Chowdhury," said Agni. "Your intention was to instigate the murder of your nephew, which is a punishable offence."

"You are disgusting, Ranjan," Shivangi screamed at Mr Chowdhury at the top of her voice. "You've been using Wajid for one disgraceful crime after another. I've been telling you repeatedly to stop using him!" She turned towards Agni and asked, "How can you be so sure that he didn't hire Wajid to kill Avigyan?"

"Well, Ms Chowdhury, your anger is justified," Agni turned towards Shivangi and smiled, "but I know for a fact that, Mr Chowdhury didn't hire Wajid for the job. It was someone else who gave Wajid the contract."

33 Unfinished Business

Night was slowly descending on the roof.

"How can you be so sure?" asked Shivangi.

Agni said, "To start with, how would Mr Chowdhury know that Avigyan would be in Kolkata on that day? For years, Avigyan had not even spoken to him. He had never informed him about his visits to Kolkata, and had never met him since the ugly spat the two of them had in Mr Chowdhury's office several years ago, over financial irregularities in the business Avigyan had been running in Mumbai.

"Wajid had been informed by the person who had hired him that Avigyan would visit someone in Salt Lake later that evening, and Avigyan was to be killed when he stepped out of the hotel. It is again unlikely that Avigyan would have discussed his plans for the night in Kolkata with Mr Chowdhury, of all persons. How would Mr Chowdhury know that Avigyan had planned to meet someone in Salt Lake that evening?

"Also, Mr Chowdhury has been working with Wajid Shamim for years now. Wajid calls him 'Maalik'. He uses Wajid to bump off anyone who comes in the way of his business interests. Wajid burns down slums for him. I'm sure there's a long list of such offences. Over the years, Wajid has been obeying his 'Maalik' without so much as batting an eyelid. The plan to kill Avigyan would have just been an addition to that long list. Why, then, would Mr Chowdhury feel the need to call Wajid from a number not known to him? And that too, in a voice that was modulated so that Wajid would not recognize the caller?

"Finally, we figured out that, Wajid had been called from a number that was registered in the name of a certain Madhav Singh from Ranchi. It had been activated a little more than two weeks before Avigyan's murder. It turned out that Madhav Singh had passed away three years back. However, his family revealed that he had been a driver in Marvel Realtors before he returned to Ranchi and died. We also came to know that after his death, Mr Chowdhury had been magnanimous enough to contact his family and send them money. The family knows Mr Chowdhury very well. Would Mr Chowdhury be stupid enough to use Madhav Singh's number, knowing fully well that the number could easily be traced to Madhav Singh and his family, then to his office, and then back to him?

"The only explanation can be that Mr Chowdhury is not the one who hired Wajid. It is someone who knows Wajid and has his contact number, but did not want to be recognized by him. Someone who knew that Avigyan would be in Kolkata that night. Someone who knew that Avigyan would leave his hotel for Salt Lake late in the evening. Someone who had access to the photo and identity proof of Madhav Singh."

"You seem to have a point there," Shivangi sat up straight and said, "Good luck with your investigation, Mr Mitra. You'll have to excuse me now, I am afraid. As you noticed, I had to leave the venue in a hurry and there are a few things that need my immediate attention."

She glared at her husband and said, "I don't want to have anything to do with this messy business anymore. I don't want to see you ever again, you fucking scumbag! The first thing I'll do tomorrow is talk to a divorce lawyer."

"Well Ms Chowdhury, you may not want to have anything to do with this messy business anymore," Agni's voice rose above the groan of the wind, "but I have unfinished business with you. We never had the chit-chat we planned this evening, remember?"

❖

Sirens bellowed at a distance. The police cars were on their way. Agni's wait was almost over.

Shivangi rolled her eyes and said, "Mr Mitra, can we get this over with quickly, please? I have allowed your colleague to search my house already, as I have nothing to hide."

Agni stood up and started walking with his arms behind him. He looked at Shivangi and smiled dryly. He said, "Ms Chowdhury, irrespective of whether you like it or not, the fact is, you got embroiled in this messy business way back in 2009, when Avigyan Chowdhury was asked to manage the Mumbai operations of your agency, Glamour Unlimited. You were spending time in Mumbai presumably to get him up to speed, introduce him to the network, to make sure that he was ready for the job. In the process, you got into a torrid relationship with him."

Agni paused.

"What the hell! Are you out of your mind?" Shivangi shouted at Agni. "He was Ranjan's nephew, for god's sake! I will not take this ridiculous slander lying down. You have no idea about my contacts. The mayor is a close friend. I can—"

Agni did not let her finish. He raised a hand and said, "Relax, Ms Chowdhury. We got Avigyan's laptop shipped to Kolkata from his rented flat in Mumbai. An examination of its hard drive revealed several videos that the mayor or you would not find particularly palatable. I would get the forensics to certify that the videos are original. I will produce them in a court of law in due time. The videos were filmed in your intimate moments with Avigyan. It does not look like you knew that you were being filmed secretly."

Shivangi's ears burnt, her face was flushed. She glanced sideways at Mr Chowdhury, who had been staring at her with dismay. She promptly looked away. Agni was not sure if she heard Mr Chowdhury muttering under his breath, "Fucking whore!"

Agni continued, "With due respect, Ms Chowdhury, you have always been heavily dependent on your husband for your finances – for the business you ran for years, and then, the NGO that you started. You like being seen in the company of the who's who of the city. The mayor is your friend. You have a status and a certain degree of respectability that you must protect. Avigyan was aware of this. He knew that you would not want those damning videos to be leaked. Those are the videos with which Avigyan blackmailed you into making a few calls to three numbers in Jharkhand. Sadly, you were left with no choice but to play along.

"Avigyan somehow managed to gather crucial information such as the phone number of the forest department bungalow where Ms Mukherjee lived with her husband, her daily habit of going to a certain place for a walk at a certain time in the morning, the fact that Siddhartha Bose would be in Netarhat a week before her birthday on 19 January that year, and would be staying at Hotel Repose.

"We don't know at this moment how he managed to gather all this information pertaining to Ms Mukherjee. Of course, it must not have been difficult for him to find out the numbers of the hotel and the nearest police station. What is important is that he had all these details at his disposal.

"You, Ms Chowdhury, were forced to travel to Mumbai, sit next to the blackmailer, and make a series of calls anonymously from a website. You called Kingshuk a few times, warning him of his wife having an affair with her friend, Siddhartha. On the morning of 20 January, you urged him to catch his wife red-handed with her lover. At the same time, you called Siddhartha, telling him that Deboleena had fallen sick near Magnolia Point. Finally, you called Pratap Jha, informing him that a terrorist had taken a couple hostage at the spot.

"Avigyan did take a few chances. What if Kingshuk did not carry a gun that morning? What if the cops did not turn up? But, I have to say, Avigyan was a great judge of human emotions. In any case, he had nothing to lose. There was no way he could be traced."

"That's a nice story, Mr Mitra. But, how will you prove any of this?" Shivangi challenged Agni.

"As you already know, Avigyan also recorded those calls you made. I recognized your voice the moment I heard the voice clips in his laptop. I got forensics to compare the voice samples in the laptop with the recording of your statement in my office. They matched.

"Ms Chowdhury, it was you whose calls dragged Kingshuk Mukherjee and Siddhartha Bose to their brutal deaths inside that forest in Netarhat ten years back."

❖

Images flashed in Shivangi's mind – the wanton nights in Avigyan's dingy bedroom in his Mira Road flat, his silence when she professed her love for him, the threats of those obscene videos getting leaked, the phone calls to Netarhat in the wee hours of the morning all through the week, then the gruesome incident on 20 January 2010 – a day she would never forget.

When Shivangi opened her eyes and looked up at Agni, her eyes were red, and her face was contorted in pain, shame and regret.

"Avigyan had with him not only the videos that would expose your affair with him, but also the voice recordings that could drag you to the gallows," Agni continued, his eyes fixed on Shivangi.

"I assume he started asking for money from you time and again to run his business in Mumbai. I had been wondering how he had managed to make ends meet in Mumbai, when Mr Chowdhury had stopped financing him and the agency had not been doing well. The simple answer to that is, he was blackmailing you. You were paying out hefty sums of money to Avigyan at regular intervals.

"You were probably finding it more and more difficult to meet his demands, which must have become unreasonable beyond a certain point. Finally, when he asked for money to start a new business, you had no choice but to turn to

Mr Chowdhury again. You asked for money and said that Avigyan had threatened to expose him over the slum fire incident. The two of you had a showdown in the office. Mr Chowdhury refused to pay him any money. When you told Avigyan about his uncle's decision, he threatened to go public with the videos and the voice recordings. You were left with no option but to silence Avigyan for good.

"You planned to finish him off."

34 | The Climax

The silence on the terrace was deafening. Shivangi had her face hidden in her palms.

"You asked Avigyan to come down to Kolkata to meet you and collect the money, in exchange for the voice recordings and the videos. You chose a date when Mr Chowdhury would be away on business. You planned to meet him late in the evening in your house at Salt Lake.

"Around the same time, you decided to hire Wajid Shamim for Avigyan's murder. You knew that he could be trusted to get the job done, though he did not come cheap. But then, you must have thought that it made more sense to hire Wajid at a high price and finish Avigyan off once and for all, rather than having to yield to Avigyan's demands every now and then.

"But you did not want to reveal your identity. So, you came up with a plan. You got a mobile phone connection in the name of Madhav Singh. You had his photograph and identity proof, which he had submitted to the office, from the time when you had briefly worked for Marvel Realtors. What you did not know was that Madhav was not just another company driver, but one of your husband's personal favourites. You did not know that your husband had reached out to his family in Jharkhand after his death, and his family had Mr Chowdhury's contact details that would lead the police to the Chowdhurys in Kolkata quite easily. Serendipity, Ms Chowdhury!

"You used that number to get in touch with Wajid, using an app to modulate your voice, so that Wajid could not even figure out if the person hiring him for murder was a man or a woman. Payments must have been arranged in such a way that you would never have had to meet Wajid in person.

"You passed on Avigyan's picture to Wajid and asked him to tail Avigyan from the moment he landed in Kolkata. Wajid was supposed to kill Avigyan when he was on his way to your residence at Salt Lake later that evening to collect the money. You had also started communicating with Avigyan about his plans in Kolkata, using the same number. We have seen the same number in call records of both Wajid and Avigyan on that day.

"What you did not know was that Ms Mukherjee had decided to meet Avigyan that evening at the hotel, invite him to her house, and murder him with an overdose of sedatives to avenge the death of her husband. Avigyan changed his plan as he did not want to miss the opportunity of being with Ms Mukherjee. Who knows? Maybe he thought of informing you later that night that he would meet you the next day.

"When Wajid saw that Avigyan had stepped out of the hotel and was headed for New Town, he called you. You instructed him to go ahead and kill him wherever it was convenient. Wajid followed your instructions. He tailed Avigyan to Ms Mukherjee's house in New Town and shot him there. No one saw him as

Ms Mukherjee and Avigyan were not in their senses. They had already consumed the pills with the wine. Wajid had no way of knowing that Avigyan would have died from the overdose in any case."

Agni paused briefly, and then said, "One more tiny detail, Ms Chowdhury. You must be wondering, how your husband came to know about what had happened at Netarhat a decade ago and informed Ms Mukherjee.

"Well, when I realized that Ms Mukherjee had poisoned Avigyan that night, I concluded that the obvious motive must have been revenge. But then, how would *she* know about the conspiracy? The police had not been able to figure out during the long trial, *who* had made those fake calls on the morning of the shootout in Netarhat. The only two persons who knew about the plan were Avigyan and you.

"So, the only possibility was that a third person had come to know about the conspiracy, possibly by overhearing conversations between Avigyan and you, and passed on the same information to Ms Mukherjee. I got your house searched and my suspicion was confirmed. Arya found out this morning that your room had been bugged."

❖

The sirens were not so distant anymore. Agni turned towards Mr Chowdhury, who could feel the bile rise up his throat and his heart pounded so hard he could hear it.

Agni said, "Mr Chowdhury, I am sure your suspicion had been aroused when you noticed Ms Chowdhury regularly withdrawing large sums of money in cash from her bank account. The last straw must have been the argument Ms Chowdhury had with you in your office, asking for money on Avigyan's behalf. You got her room bugged, and overheard conversations where they discussed the incident at Ranchi, and Avigyan blackmailing Ms Chowdhury for years. That was how you got the information that you then used to your advantage to incite the murder of Avigyan. Am I right, Mr Chowdhury?"

Mr Chowdhury sighed and slowly nodded, not bothering to look at Agni.

"Ms Chowdhury, you cannot hold me responsible for divulging the truth about your dark past to your husband," Agni said, looking in the direction of Shivangi. "He had come to know it all from your conversations with Avigyan." Shivangi had not spoken a word and still had her face hidden. Agni could see her shoulders shaking and could hear her sobs.

Agni looked away and ran his fingers through his hair ruffled by the warm breeze, when suddenly, from the corner of his eyes, he saw a flash of green, bolting past the two men. He turned around and saw that Shivangi was already near the edge of the terrace. Mr Chowdhury, who was closer, stood up and walked briskly towards his wife. He was just in time to grab Shivangi's hand as she jumped over the railing.

It seemed to Mr Chowdhury that his wife's impulsive act had suddenly transported him to a position of advantage. He slurred, "Mr Mitra, let me go! Or else, she dies!" Agni trained his gun at Mr Chowdhury, taken over suddenly by a sense of déjà vu.

The roof of a skyscraper, his gun pointing at a demented malefactor, whose slippery hand was the only thing between the woman dangling several hundred feet above the ground and her imminent death. Agni had been living that moment in his nightmares for years now.

Agni could see the madness in Mr Chowdhury's eyes.

"You really think you can shoot me, Mr Mitra?" Mr Chowdhury shouted defiantly. "Let me go! You know I wouldn't think twice before letting the slut fall to a miserable death!"

Agni inched ahead, the wind whistling in his ears just the way it did in his dreams. He had found himself in that nightmare for years, but he would not let this end the same way.

Agni could see Shivangi's eyes, the silent plea in them. She had wanted to take her own life, but right at that moment, dangling in mid-air, grasping the hand of a man who had neither love nor respect left for her, she was staring at almost inevitable death, and suddenly she did not want to die.

"Pull her up!" Agni ordered, the gun pointing at Mr Chowdhury's forehead. The relentless cries of Shivangi cut through the silence of the night.

The sirens stopped, and before long, Agni could hear heavy boots on the stairs leading to the terrace. He could see Shivangi's fingers slowly slipping, and Mr Chowdhury laughed as if he had lost his sanity.

"Avigyan deserved to die, Mr Mitra," he kept yelling. "He was an incompetent, ungrateful son-of-a-bitch who came to me asking for favours and then looted my money, slept with my wife, kept blackmailing her for years, and had the guts to blackmail *me*!"

He stopped to breathe and went on, "But more than him, it's this bitch here who should burn in hell! I indulged her whims and fancies for years, I met all her demands without so much as asking a question, and she chose to fuck my nephew, splurge my money, and lie to me for years! I have been wanting to kill her since the day I came to know what she had been up to behind my back."

Agni saw from the corner of his eyes that Arya was on the roof with the other officers, and they had taken aim at Mr Chowdhury. He lunged forward and grabbed Shivangi's wrist, just as Mr Chowdhury had started taking his hand off.

"This has to end differently," Agni kept reminding himself as he started pulling Shivangi up, inch by inch. By then, the police had already surrounded Ranjan Chowdhury on all sides. Arya was putting the handcuffs on him.

❖

Agni and Arya returned to Archana after Shivangi and Mr Chowdhury had been taken away. She was waiting for them, applying an ice pack on her bruised lips.

"Your nightmare is over, Archana." Agni said. "I'm sorry that you fell in love with the wrong man. Your trust was misplaced."

"I guess I was destined to learn my lessons the hard way," she tried to smile, and the pain immediately made her grimace. But she continued, "I…I'm happy that it was *you* who was meant to show me the way."

"We need to do something about *that*." Agni pointed at Archana's lips and said, "Let me take you to a clinic."

Archana nodded hesitantly.

"What is it?" asked Agni.

"Just one thing before we leave," Archana said, taking a few steps towards Agni. She hugged him tightly and buried her face in his chest, whispering, "Thank you for saving my life. You will forever be my hero."

Agni could not decide what to do with his hands. He glanced sideways at Arya, who cleared his throat, tried to suppress a smile, and walked away shaking his head.

Epilogue

Deboleena Mukherjee

It had taken Deboleena some effort to keep her grief and anger buried in a hidden chamber in the depths of her heart and move on with life. When she performed on stage, when she taught music to kids in schools, when she appeared before the media, or when she discussed business contracts with music companies, her smile, her indefatigable spirit, and her energy that she owed to her love for music were all that were there for the world to see.

There was no room for sympathy or a painful reminder of her past from anyone around her even if the intentions behind them were sincere.

On those odd nights, she allowed herself to cry when she was alone in her room, listening to songs of yesteryears which reminded her of the beautiful moments she had spent with Kingshuk. The wind played with the lacey curtains of her room, carrying with them from someplace unknown strange fragrances that seemed so familiar, the wine gradually numbed the pain that otherwise found expression only in her music.

Deboleena was, therefore, shocked when Ranjan Chowdhury, an infamous builder whose name had come up a few years back in connection with an incident of a slum being burnt down, almost coaxed her into meeting him to discuss 'the incident at Netarhat ten years back'.

What could he possibly know about the tragedy that had changed her life forever? What information would he have access to, when the police had failed to solve the puzzle after years of investigation? Those were the questions uppermost in her mind. Her curiosity, however, got the better of her, and she found herself giving in to his request. They met at his club.

Deboleena had always suspected that the tragedy had not been a case of human error, but there had been a sinister conspiracy that had brought Kingshuk, Siddhartha, the police and her at the same place, at the same time, under circumstances that had been open to a variety of interpretations, eventually leading to the police killing Kingshuk and Kingshuk killing Siddhartha.

Mr Chowdhury mentioned that his nephew Avigyan Chowdhury and his wife Shivangi Chowdhury had been behind the conspiracy. Avigyan had hatched the plot and Shivangi had assisted him in carrying it out. Shivangi was the one who had been calling Kingshuk every other morning that week to tell him that his wife was having a clandestine affair with Siddhartha.

Shivangi was the one who had called Siddhartha that morning to tell him that Deboleena had fallen sick near Magnolia Point. Shivangi was the one who had called the police to tell them that a terrorist had been seen holding a couple hostage at the place where Kingshuk had been told to go and catch his wife and her friend red-handed.

Deboleena's first reaction was not to trust the man. She allowed her judgment to be clouded by the man's reputation. To her surprise, Mr Chowdhury apparently had foreseen such a possibility. Mr Chowdhury made Deboleena listen to telephonic conversations between his wife and his nephew, the two perpetrators of the crime, which he had recorded. He had no scruples in admitting that he had got his wife's room bugged. His nephew had recorded Shivangi's calls and had been blackmailing her for years. He was now demanding more money to start a new business by threatening Mr Chowdhury. Mr Chowdhury was not going to let them get away. The wife had asked the nephew to come down to Kolkata and had promised that she would try to arrange for the money.

Deboleena patiently listened to hours of conversations. On different days, the two had talked about different parts of the story, and it was not too difficult to put the pieces of the puzzle together. Deboleena was finally convinced.

❖

For a few days, Deboleena could not make up her mind what she should do with the truth that she had been desperate to unearth ten years back. She wondered if she should go to the police. And then, she remembered the years she spent in police stations and court rooms, repeating herself over and over again till she had no energy left, witnessing the law taking its own serpentine course that went nowhere, experiencing despair and hopelessness completely overwhelm her. She did not want to walk down the same road again.

It might be easier if she chose to deliver by herself the justice that Kingshuk had been denied. She knew that she needed closure. Because ever since she had come to know the truth, absolutely nothing could contain the blind rage that coursed through her veins. Neither the music nor the fragrances from days left behind were of any help. In fact, they stabbed into wounds she thought had long been healed and drew fresh blood. The wine left her thirsty for vengeance, instead of putting her to sleep.

Mr Chowdhury had offered to help her. She had thanked him and bade him farewell. It was her battle, and she would fight it alone. She was not going to rely on someone like Mr Chowdhury, who, she suspected, must have had an ulterior motive behind sharing the truth with her.

She wondered whether she should meet her brother, Debesh Roy, and tell him everything. Debesh, the proverbial black sheep of the family, was a patient of chronic depression himself. He had distanced himself from their father's business, set up his own, and was now struggling. His family had abandoned him when he had needed them the most. Would it be right to burden him with her dilemma?

But then, he was the only family she had left. He had every right to know.

❖

Mr Roy wanted Deboleena to go to the police. She refused and explained to him why. She told him about the plan that had been taking shape in her mind. She would meet Avigyan and then, kill him with an overdose of sedatives in his drink. Mr Roy wanted to know more details. He wanted to know how Deboleena would dispose of the body. He wanted to know how she would manage to escape. He was worried about Deboleena's safety around the ruthless man who had got her husband murdered. Deboleena was not going to give him the details. She asked him to be strong and to trust her instincts. He eventually gave up trying.

The fact that Deboleena was several years younger than him had never come in the way of his respecting her judgment. She had always been the strong one, who had had her way with the family.

Avigyan Chowdhury

It took me a while to believe my eyes when a message from Deboleena Mukherjee flashed on Messenger.

For years, I had resisted the temptation to follow Deboleena on Facebook. I had not had the nerve to see her basking in the warmth of happy matrimony. In fact, I had spent years thinking that my hatred for Deboleena would be satiated only if I could cause grievous harm to her.

Then I went ahead and got her husband killed. I got her friend killed. I began to believe that the shootout at Netarhat must have broken her. It was only after that incident that I started stalking her on Facebook, hoping to rejoice in her misery.

But, contrary to what I had expected, she managed to emerge stronger from the tragedy. She returned to Kolkata, carved out a career in singing, cut albums, started her own YouTube channel that had a very large number of followers.

However, irrespective of what the happy pictures on Facebook kept telling me, I wondered if, in the deep recesses of her heart, she had really been able to move on. I knew how much she loved Kingshuk and I wondered if one could put that kind of love behind and get on with life.

So, when Deboleena messaged me saying that she had seen my profile on Facebook and wanted to check if I was the same "guy from college who wrote letters to her at the address of the English Department", I did not know how to respond.

Truth be told, my pulse raced, and my heart leapt into my throat when I saw her message. For the first time ever, Deboleena had initiated a conversation with me, albeit virtually.

My eagerness to come closer to the woman I had loved and hated all my life with all my heart, won over my apprehension about getting in touch with the woman whose husband and friend I had got killed. Love makes you do crazy things!

We got talking. We ended up exchanging phone numbers. By some magic, my hatred for Deboleena was beginning to wear off, revealing what it really was at the core – love that knew no bounds.

I was planning to visit Kolkata. Shivangi had promised to arrange for money, even though my uncle had refused to pay a dime. She wanted me to delete the videos and the voice recordings for good. We planned to meet at her Salt Lake residence. Her husband would be away that night.

Deboleena and I planned to meet in the evening.

Deboleena Mukherjee

Deboleena had never been to Hotel Paradise. One look at the hotel and she knew it was just the kind of place where someone like Avigyan would put up – cheap, shady and dodgy.

As Deboleena's car stopped in front of the hotel, a part of her wanted to run away. Another part of her reminded her that she did not have a choice. She had agreed to meet Avigyan at the hotel in the evening. That was the night she had been looking forward to for weeks. Deboleena braced herself for the evening. She had to act like someone from the opposite pole – single, independent, rich, and on the lookout for new friends and good times.

She was approached by the valet, and got out of the car. She called Avigyan as she walked into the hotel. He said that he was waiting for her at the bar upstairs. She went to the reception desk and asked the man there for directions to the bar. Deboleena felt his dirty gaze on her, as she made her way to the elevator.

She stepped out of the elevator and walked towards the bar. It was semi-lit in cheap, bluish light, instrumental versions of Bollywood numbers playing in high volume. The live band advertised outside was yet to start playing and Deboleena was not complaining. A man in white shirt and black trousers, his tummy protruding through an ill-fitting black coat, approached her. Deboleena looked around and could immediately recognize Avigyan, sitting in a corner of the room, checking his watch anxiously.

For a few seconds, Deboleena stood there, staring at him. Here was the beast who had taken away from her the only man she had ever loved, and changed her life forever. She wanted to pounce on him right there and strangle him till his last breath abandoned him. Her heart thumped loudly against her ribs and she balled her fist.

"Is it just you, ma'am?" the query from the usher brought Deboleena back to her senses. She ignored him and made her way towards Avigyan.

Avigyan stood up as soon as he saw Deboleena and grinned. Even in the dim light, Deboleena did not miss the expression of gratitude on Avigyan's face. As if Deboleena had done him a favour just by turning up. The man had hardly changed since the time she had seen him last in college. The years had been kind to his natural good looks. But he still looked somewhat unsure and desperate and he still did not make eye contact.

There was something in those furtive eyes which told that he was not a man who could be trusted. Deboleena wondered if the cheap, ill-fitting blazer was an attempt to make himself look classy.

Avigyan ordered the cheapest whiskey on the menu and tried to make small talk. Over the next ninety minutes, amidst long spells of awkward silence, he asked Deboleena about her family with a straight face and Deboleena told him about the shootout in Netarhat at which he expressed his fake sympathies. He tried very hard to convince Deboleena that they had a shared love for art – she was a singer and his agency, which Deboleena had never heard of, groomed fresh talent. When the whiskey had helped him loosen up a bit, he said that he was lonely just like Deboleena, and finally, made a half-hearted attempt at telling Deboleena that he had had "special feelings for her" for close to seventeen years, since the time he had first seen her in the college fest.

When Deboleena felt that she had sat through the circus long enough, she looked at her watch and said that she had had a lovely time in Avigyan's company, and had ended up drinking more than she usually did. She added that it would be most kind of him if he could drive her home.

She did not miss the glint in the eyes of the bastard.

AVIGYAN CHOWDHURY

I sat in Deboleena's bedroom, as she went away to freshen up and make drinks for us.

I wondered if this was a dream.

I had never been closer to the woman I loved. I had never felt luckier, never felt more blessed. I was feeling alive, like I had never felt before. This was my moment, our moment – one that I had wanted with all my heart ever since the day when I had seen and heard her inside that auditorium in college.

I would not be just a guest for the night. I wanted to live that night to the fullest. I wanted to tell her everything that I had always wanted to. I wanted to listen to her, to wipe away the tears which I had given her in return for the ones she had given me.

Maybe I would tell her about the day when I came to know that she was getting married to Kingshuk, the day when I drank for the first time, the day I was robbed and kicked out by the hotel staff and found myself crying alone in a park in the middle of the night, the day I started hating her. Should I also confess that I had got her husband and her friend killed? Maybe not yet!

I wondered if I would find the right words, when she stood in front of me right inside this room, which suddenly felt small, with its walls closing in on me. I could feel myself getting drawn all over again into the ocean of love and hope and dreams that surrounded me during the days when I secretly followed her around in the campus.

I wondered if she would ask me to stay back, when the day dawned. And then, I told myself that I would be happy even if she just said that she would never forget me and the night that we spent together. That would be enough for me.

I could feel the tears streaming down my cheeks. For the first time in years, I thanked my god.

Shivangi and her money could wait for another day.

Deboleena Mukherjee

Deboleena got the bottle of her sleeping pills from the kitchen cabinet and emptied it on the bar counter. She then sat at the bar, crushing the pills down into fine dust on the counter, to be added to the two glasses of wine which she had poured just a while back.

Deboleena smiled to herself. Her brother had asked her what her escape plan was. He had no idea. Over the last couple of weeks, Deboleena had tried to figure out what she would do with her life once Kingshuk's murder was avenged. She had come to realize that without her knowing it, she had been living with the sole purpose of getting herself justice, and the closure she so badly needed.

The man sitting in the next room would be dead very soon. With his death, life would suddenly have no purpose left. She might as well draw the curtains on her own miserable life. She felt exhausted.

Deboleena thought about the man she was about to kill. She remembered the boy who stammered every time they came face to face in the campus, who waited outside the examination hall to wish her luck, who followed her around the campus and wrote stupid love letters in raw English he never had the guts to deliver himself.

What was he thinking right now? Was he thinking that this was going to be his lucky night? Was he thinking that Deboleena would be with him for the rest of his life from this moment on?

Deboleena could not help but feel a hint of sadness in some corner of her heart. She was struggling to be the monster she wanted herself to be that night. But being a monster did not come to Deboleena easily.

She sighed. Her eyes went to Kingshuk's picture that hung on the opposite wall. Those bright eyes filled with dreams, those lips that had only words of love and kindness for her, those broad shoulders that were meant to be her support for a lifetime.

Then, she remembered the last moments of the same man, bullets in his back, writhing in pain at her feet on the dust, angry and broken over a misunderstanding that made him hate her in his final moments, as life slowly ebbed away. She wanted him to take her in a hug as she set out now to do what she had never imagined in her wildest dreams.

Deboleena had not realized when the tears had started streaming down her cheeks. But that was not the moment to shed tears.

She wiped her tears away and put the glasses on the drinks trolley along with the bottle of wine, and a plate filled with cashew nuts. She headed for the bedroom and then, stopped to turn around and look at Kingshuk one last time.